N

Swopping the greyness of England for sunny Spain seemed like a dream come true for Nurse Hilary Wilson. The only snag came when she discovered that the bossy man she had met on the beach was none other than the distinguished Dr Steve Sanders . . . and he too was working at the hospital for English patients.

Rhona Trezise was brought up in Cornwall. On her marriage to an architect she moved to London where they had a son and daughter. In 1967 she started writing short stories for women's magazines and the BBC, as well as picture scripts for teenagers and articles for educational journals. Having spent some time as a patient in various hospitals, she was so impressed by the loving care and charm of the nurses and doctors that she was prompted to weave romances around them. She obtains her medical information from many friends in the profession and from textbooks and medical journals.

Nurse in the Sun is Rhona Trezise's seventh Doctor Nurse Romance. Recent titles include *Deborah and Dr Carr, Nurse Hannah* and *Suzanne and the Doctor*.

NURSE IN THE SUN

BY

RHONA TREZISE

MILLS & BOON PTY. LIMITED
SYDNEY · AUCKLAND · MANILA
LONDON · TORONTO

First published in Great Britain 1987
by Mills & Boon Limited
First Australian paperback edition August 1987

ISBN 0 263 75743 9

Printed in Australia by
The Book Printer,
North Blackburn, Victoria 3130

CHAPTER ONE

HILARY opened one sleepy blue eye, looked around her bedroom and didn't like what she saw. There was a greyness about everything, the unmistakable spatter of rain on the window pane and a decided chill in the air. Duvets were fine in Spain, but here at home she was glad of her sheets and blankets. She pulled them higher around her neck and nuzzled her head in the pillow. Bed was the best place today.

To think that for the last three weeks she had been lying on a sun-bed on a sandy beach in Spain, wearing only a bikini and sun-tan oil, feeling the heat of the sun seeping into her and hopefully toasting her skin to a delectable shade of brown. It had been bliss, until that man had approached her.

She had seen him before on many occasions; he was the sort of person you couldn't disregard, he looked so different from the usual run of holidaymakers, especially the Englishmen, who could often be recognised by their sandals, socks and over-long shorts. He was exceedingly up-market—she would swear his tailored slacks and immaculate cream shirt had never been in direct contact with the sand. His bearing was aristocratic and as he strolled along the beach she watched his every step. Just in case he should notice her she made a point of lying gracefully and making sure her hair was not untidy. But apart from occasionally giving her a brief glance in passing he seemed completely uninterested. Until the day before yesterday.

On that occasion Hilary knew she was looking her best, for her skin had become a glowing shade of gold and she was wearing a sky-blue bikini with a scalloped edge and had tied her hair into a ponytail with a ribbon to match. She saw him approaching, walking leisurely with a hand slipped casually into his pocket. He glanced at her briefly, then turned away and stood looking out at the sparkling green waves. He ran a hand over his well-trimmed dark brown hair as if undecided about something. He started to walk away, then suddenly swung around and came towards her. With a throb of pleasurable excitement she gave him a welcoming smile and raised her hand to shield her eyes from the sun the better to see him.

He was even better looking seen close to. His dark blue eyes immediately sent a thrill through her, for they had a disturbing expression in them, an intensity and a warmth and were framed with thick, dark, curling lashes. He was not particularly sunburnt but looked naturally healthy and had a sexy, well-shaped mouth.

'Hello,' said Hilary with a welcoming smile.

He gave a brief unsmiling nod. 'Good

morning. A word of warning to you,' he said stiffly.

Her smile faded. She looked hastily at her bikini to check if any part of it had come adrift, but all was well.

'Of warning?' she repeated. Was her sun-bed in danger of collapsing?

'Yes indeed. It isn't good to lie out in the sun as much as you've been doing, especially when you have such fair skin.' He spoke as if he was a lecturer addressing a schoolgirl.

She felt inordinately snubbed, and disappointed too, for she had thought he was admiring her when he looked her way—instead he was criticising. How dared he! She hadn't asked for his advice and he had no right at all to give it. She certainly wasn't going to take it.

Looking at him condescendingly and stifling a yawn, she said,

'One gets used to the climate in time, you'll see.'

As the pupils of his eyes appeared to contract they took on a steely glint.

'Lying in the sun too much can give you skin cancer whether you're accustomed to it or not.' He sounded positively dictatorial.

She gave an unamused laugh. 'Oh dear, so you're one of those tiresome people who believes that anything that gives you pleasure is bad for you! I wondered what type of people they were.'

His mouth tightened at the corners. 'Cancer is not a laughing matter,' he said brusquely.

Hilary rolled over on to her side and so turned her back on him. 'Well, if I get skin cancer that'll be no skin off your nose,' she said too sweetly. Immediately she felt disgusted with herself for her crude remark and swung around with the intention of somehow making amends, but already he was walking away, and she hadn't seen him again.

There was the sound of movement from the other bed in the room. A girl yawned loudly and asked indistinctly,

'Are you awake?'

Hilary groaned inwardly. There wasn't going to be any more peace, she knew that.

'No,' she mumbled.

'How was everything? Did you have a good time?'

She grunted and burrowed deeper in the bed.

'Oh, come on, don't be mean! I'm longing to hear all about it.' Tessa sat up in bed in her candy-pink baby-doll nightdress and ran her fingers through corn-coloured spiky hair.

'Isn't it time you were leaving for work?' asked Hilary.

'Ha, ha! So we're pretending we've got jet-lag, are we? Clot! It's Sunday, thank the Lord.'

Hilary rolled over and stared at the ceiling, which was nothing like the blue Spanish sky but off-white and etched with cracks.

'What have you brought me back?' asked Tessa.

'Have a heart, I haven't unpacked yet.

Anyhow, what makes you think I've brought you anything?'

'Because I'm your poor hard-working sister who's never been abroad in her life.'

'I'll show you something that'll make you green with envy. Take a look at that.' Hilary turned back a sheet and lifted her pyjama jacket.

Tessa whistled silently. 'Lucky you, it's super!'

Hilary wrinkled her nose. 'It isn't much use to me now. Who's going to see it under my uniform?'

Tessa chuckled. 'There's only one answer to that. Do a spot of streaking.'

Hilary's eyes sparkled. 'That's a smashing idea. I could streak across Men's Medical ward, and I can just imagine old man Rhodes——'

The sentence died away as she remembered that she'd left the hospital now that she had passed her SRN exams and had to move away to find a job elsewhere. There were no vacancies in the Memorial Hospital for newly qualified staff nurses. 'It's too late, I'm now one of the unemployed,' she said ruefully.

'Never mind about that. Did you meet anyone exciting? You must have done, I don't believe you spent three weeks on your own.' But even as she spoke Tessa thought it was quite possible that Hilary would have done just that. 'Did you?' she ended doubtfully.

Hilary immediately thought of the bossy blue-eyed man and mentally thumbed her nose at him, because he hadn't been the only pebble on the beach. There was Nick Trowbridge who was completely different, yet very handsome too, with blond hair that curled around his ears and neck, and mischievous brown eyes under straight brows. He wore fun clothes, tee-shirts, baggy pants, sneakers and lots of gold chains and bracelets that sparkled against his sun-tanned skin.

'Yes, I met a really dishy man who was just up your street,' she told her sister.

'Really?' Tessa's eyes gleamed. 'Tell me more! Right from the beginning, like where you first met.' She leaned back against her pillows and waited expectantly.

Hilary's thoughts went back to the start of her holiday when she stood on the sandy beach feeling she looked like a partly peeled banana with her yellow bikini against her white skin. The sand was delightfully warm to her feet and when she put a toe tentatively in the wave that slowly rolled towards her she quickly withdrew it. 'Not today, Josephine, I'm going to lie in the sun,' she said to herself.

Suddenly strong arms gripped her waist and she spun around with a gasp to see a bronzed Amazon laughing at her from wicked brown eyes.

'You're on your way, honey,' he said, and ran with her into the sea, the water splashing up and over them.

She squealed and struggled, but he dunked her, then held her close against his hairy chest until she regained her breath.

'That wasn't too bad, was it?' His face, sparkling with drops of water, was but inches from her own.

'N—no,' she gasped, unable to be angry with such an attractive, friendly man. 'But you shouldn't have done that. Say I hadn't wanted to go in the sea?'

'Then I would have apologised and to make amends invited you to have a drink with me. I'll do that anyhow. And you'll be able to tell your friends back home that you've been bathing with an Olympic swimmer.'

'Are you really?' Hilary's blue eyes opened wide with awe.

'Now do I look like a man who'd lie to you?'

Looking at his mischievous eyes she thought he quite likely did.

'I met him on the beach,' she told Tessa now.

'And did you see him much afterwards?'

Hilary nodded. 'Quite often. He wanted me to stay on over there and work for him.'

Tessa laughed unbelievingly. 'So he ran a brothel?'

Hilary felt under the bed and picking up a slipper hurled it at her sister. She missed, of course.

'As a matter of fact he was an extremely successful estate agent. And—pin back your lug-holes—he had a silver-grey Merc.'

'You're kidding,' Tessa protested.

'I'm not.'

'Then why on earth didn't you take him up on his offer?'

'Do you know, I wondered that myself. But after all those years of slogging at my exams —well, it would be an awful waste, wouldn't it? And what would Mum and Dad have said?'

Tessa rolled her eyes heavenwards. 'It doesn't bear thinking about. But they'd have got over it in time. And anyhow, it's your life, for goodness' sake.'

'I admit it was very tempting——'

'But you being you, you wouldn't take the plunge, I suppose. How we came to be sisters I can't imagine!'

Hilary looked wistfully at the rain-spattered window. 'I often wish I was more like you, I'm sure you get more fun out of life.'

'You can say that again! Mine isn't exactly fun-packed, but compared with yours——'

'Mine's not so bad, I really like nursing. Well, I will do now those beastly exams are out of the way. But if it isn't one thing it's another. I've got to try and get a job now, and despite what Mum thinks vacancies aren't thick on the ground.'

Tessa yawned and stretched. 'Each to his own—I'd loathe nursing. Most of all I'd hate to have to wear that old uniform every day. I'm not madly keen on working in the supermarket, but at least I can wear what I like and can speak to people who are hale and hearty.'

'New clothes don't bother me. I'd hate to

have to wonder every day what to put on. It's easier to shove on the old uniform. And as I haven't got to buy them I can afford a holiday which will give me a tan like this,' Hilary said cruelly, lifting her pyjama jacket again.

'You've got a nasty nature, cruel and unkind,' Tessa said amiably, and jumped out of bed with a thud which would have done the ceiling below no good at all.

Putting a foot in Hilary's slipper, she hopped to the window and pulling back the curtain looked out at the leaden sky and sodden grass.

'It seems to have stopped raining, let's go for a walk after breakfast, then you can tell me all about your holiday. Talking of which, what have you brought me back?'

'No rest for the wicked,' sighed Hilary as she climbed unwillingly out of bed. As her foot touched the cold linoleum she let out a yell.

'You've got my slipper! Give it back or I won't get up.'

'I'll swop you. Your slipper for my pressy.'

'Okay. Slipper first.'

As she bent to open her suitcase she felt a momentary sadness. When she had finished unpacking that would be the end of the only holiday she'd ever had, and it would be many years before she could afford another. It would be good to tell Tessa all about it, because she didn't want the memory to fade too soon.

'Here you are, I hope you like it.' She handed

Tessa a carrier-bag emblazoned with the name of a Spanish store.

Tessa took it with a pleased smile, peeped inside, then lifted out a black silk blouse richly embroidered with red and pink flowers.

'It's beautiful,' she said excitedly, holding it against her. 'I've just bought a super black skirt with a slit up the side and it'll look great over that. Thanks a lot, Hilary.'

Hilary thought back to the day she had bought it in one of the shops which catered chiefly for tourists. Nick had taken her there and had bought her a soft pale blue suede purse which would never withstand the workaday life it would be subjected to, but it was lovely, and she stroked it now admiringly. Had she been foolish not to stay in Spain with him?

'And live on air?' she'd said when he asked her.

He'd stretched and yawned widely. 'Not entirely, you'd have a job with me.'

She'd looked at him dubiously. 'What sort of a job?'

He crossed his legs and laced his hands behind his head. 'Anything you like.'

When she looked unconvinced he said, 'Only a moron would swop the pleasant life I'm offering for being stuck in a grotty old hospital day after day. And I didn't know that morons came gift-wrapped in golden hair, sky-blue eyes and a cracking figure.'

Never before had anyone said such exciting

things to her, and she loved it.

'Flatterer!' she laughed. 'You could almost persuade me with that sort of talk. But seriously, nursing is my job and it's what I've spent an awful long time working at and studying to get my exams. I can't just throw all that away.'

His eyes formed two mischievous slits. 'No need, honey, you can nurse me any time you like!'

She knew that he was not the type of man to be taken seriously, but why, oh, why did she always have to be so cautious? Tessa would do whatever she wanted even if she regretted it later.

She was putting foundation cream on her face when she felt the roughness on her nose. Bending forward, she peered closer in the mirror, then let out a cry of dismay.

'Oh no! My nose is peeling!'

If it didn't serve her right after what she had said to 'that man'. Maybe it was no skin off *his* nose, but it certainly was off her own. Thank heavens he would never know, or how he would gloat. She could just picture the satisfaction, that smug look in those blue eyes. He would stand and look down at her, his body, large and commanding, close to hers and—at the thought a delicious tremor trickled through her body—he would reach out and stroke her nose with his long, well-manicured forefinger.

'What's up? Did a ghost walk over your grave?' Tessa stared at her with curiosity.

'No, I—I shivered. It's cold after Spain.'

'That's right, rub it in,' grunted Tessa. 'You know darned well I'll never be able to go there.'

After breakfast when they went for their walk and Tessa was full of questions Hilary answered her, but over and over again her thoughts turned to 'that man'. Who and what was he? He neither looked like a resident nor a holidaymaker, but was more likely the latter. Possibly the headmaster of an expensive public school brushing up on Spanish architecture. He looked that sort of person, clever and bossy and used to being obeyed. What puzzled her was why he had bothered to speak to her. He hadn't wanted to pick her up, he preferred to put her down. He had obviously taken her for a first-time visitor, and she wondered why. Was it so obvious? With a spurt of indignation she felt glad that she had spoken as she did. And yet if she had smiled and taken his advice gratefully would he perhaps have sat beside her? Would they have become friends? The possibility was delightful, but she had to admit it was merely wishful thinking, for clearly they came from different worlds.

Monday came and things were back to normal. Tessa had set off for work wearing her new blouse and skirt, her hair more outrageous even than usual. Their father had left much earlier for his job as a gardener. Hilary went into the kitchen and picking up a cloth began to wipe the breakfast dishes.

'What are you going to do today?' her mother

asked, drying her soapy hands on a towel.

'Like it or not, I've got to look for a job,' said Hilary. 'And it isn't going to be easy. If I'd had any sense I'd have started applying as soon as my results came through, that's when all the jobs come and go.'

'Well, never mind, love,' Mrs Wilson said fondly. 'You deserved a holiday and you enjoyed it, and I'm glad. You'll find something, you'll see.'

In her pride at Hilary's success in her chosen career she believed that no nurse could compete with her in any way, that hospital administrators up and down the country would all be clamouring for her services, but Hilary knew better.

'I can only hope so. I thought I'd have a look through the papers and see what's on offer.'

She put on a blue anorak, took a notebook and pen, and set off for the public library. Men, chiefly, sat in the armchairs either dozing or with newspapers open in front of them, while upstairs students sat at the tables with textbooks and papers and were strangely silent. Hilary took some nursing newspapers from the book rack and found a vacant chair. She opened her notebook and put it on her knee ready to write in it a list of possible vacancies, but even after the clock on the wall showed her that an hour and a half had elapsed she had only entered two, neither of which appealed to her. One was with a family who was moving to Saudi Arabia and required an English nurse for their four children. The other was for a nurse in a private nursing home in the Scilly Isles. She had no desire to go to Saudi where she believed it would be very hot, and she didn't wholly approve of private nursing homes. But she would have to try for something, and if no nursing vacancy cropped up then she would take any job at all rather than be a burden to her parents. If she was not nursing, though, she would have done better to have taken up Nick's offer and stayed in Spain. She could go back—on second thoughts she couldn't, because she didn't have the fare.

As she was replacing the papers she picked up a copy of *The Lady*, which had a situations vacant column. They certainly had some very interesting ones today, and she was tempted to apply for several off-beat ones when a word which was familiar caught her eye. Finola. That was the place she had just returned from. She read the advertisement with interest. An SRN was required for an English hospital in Spain. Someone—Nick?—must be playing a trick on her. Well, trick or not she was going to apply for it. Not that she held out much hope of getting it, but how wonderful it would be if she did.

She walked home through the park which she knew so well. She had always enjoyed this walk, first of all going to and from school, then later to the bus stop which took her to the hospital.

Every season of the year brought new delights, even winter when snowdrops and crocuses pushed their tiny brave heads through thawing snow; in spring when the trees were covered with blossom and sprouting green leaves; in summer when roses climbed over the old brick walls and the flower-beds were a riot of colour, and almost best of all in autumn when leaves were crisp on the ground and chestnuts burst from their prickly cases and the trees were breathtakingly beautiful in yellows and rust and brown.

At the far end of the park was a lake, and on Saturdays when they were young she and Tessa used to go there to feed the ducks and admire the graceful swans that nested on an island in the middle and which, on occasion, would sail proudly across it with a trail of cygnets in their wake. Nearby in a clearing were piles of logs and a bonfire which sent up thin spirals of smoke. No wonder her father loved his work!

They lived in one of a row of small cottages at the entrance to the park. All were occupied by park workers. The larger, detached house, set a little apart from the others, was for the head gardener, but Hilary's father didn't aspire to that position. He had no wish to deal with any paperwork or tell others what to do, he just wanted to dig and plant and watch the plants grow. Her mother, too, was not ambitious, except for Hilary, and her pride in her was immense. But for herself she was happy to work as a cleaner and part-time dinner lady at the nearby primary school. Hilary believed it would be impossible to find any two people who had more job satisfaction than her parents. It was strange that some people got their pleasure from striving to get the apples from the top of a tree while others rejoiced in picking up the windfalls.

As for herself, she had loved having the praise of her parents when she came top of the class at school, and it was chiefly to please them that she had taken up nursing, only to find that she believed nothing could have given her more pleasure, especially as she had been able to live at home during training, for they were a loving and united family.

Now, however, Hilary knew that she would have to move away, probably not to Spain, but definitely somewhere, and she felt sad. She would miss her parents and Tessa and her walks through the park.

CHAPTER TWO

AFTER what seemed like months but was only seven weeks Hilary was called for an interview for the vacancy in Finola. It was held in a small hotel in London, and four other nurses were also hopefully waiting.

'Yes, I know the area well and I like it immensely,' Hilary said to the interviewer.

Whether or not it was because of that piece of exaggeration, she was later offered the job and was delighted to accept. Her mother wasn't so pleased.

'I 'd rather you hadn't got to go so far away. We'll miss you,' she said unhappily.

'I'll have my holidays home here with you, Mum,' Hilary said.

'Goody! I'll have my bedroom all to myself,' gloated Tessa. But she added seriously, 'Get me a job out there if you can.'

Mr Wilson as usual said nothing, merely smiled as if he was pleased.

Ten days later Hilary boarded the plane at Heathrow, leaving behind sunshine and showers and gale force winds. When she landed at Malaga airport she felt as if she had stepped straight into an oven. A more seasoned traveller would have known not to wear a padded anorak. But because of her recent holiday she knew where to find a trolley for her luggage and where amongst the milling crowds she could get a taxi.

The short journey from the airport to Finola was attractively foreign-looking, with white buildings decorated with wrought-iron railings to the steps and the balconies and with arches cut into the plaster.

Half hidden by grey-green trees, opposite the restaurant which she and Nick had frequented, was a rose-red brick building which she knew was the hospital. The taxi slowed down as it neared the drive that led to the entrance and a man took this opportunity to cross the road. He walked purposefully, and something familiar about his bearing made Hilary's heart leap. Was it 'that man'? Oh yes, it was him all right, and he was no doubt on his way to tell some poor unsuspecting person that what they were doing was wrong. She twisted round in her seat to watch him as he walked, head in air, looking down his aristocratic nose as if he owned the place. And yes, he probably did! He was no doubt the owner of the restaurant, not just this one, of course. Oh no! Most likely a whole string of them all over Spain.

The taxi sped up the tree-lined drive and stopped outside the hospital. The driver got out and dumped her luggage on the steps, then drove away. Hilary stood looking around at the sunny scene and felt overwhelmingly happy.

And only to herself would she have admitted that it was because 'that man' was still in the vicinity. Though why that should please her she had no idea.

She pushed open the door and looked around. There was a marble-floored circular area with doors leading off it and it looked more like a private nursing home or hotel than a hospital, and she didn't know where to go.

Seeing a middle-aged man in a brown uniform jacket, she asked him if he could help her, speaking slowly and clearly and hoping he could understand English.

'Help you? Yes, miss. What can I do you for?' he asked in a cheerful cockney voice.

She gave a smile of relief. 'Thank goodness you know what I'm talking about! I've come here to work as a nurse. Where should I go?'

'That's no problem—walk this way.' He gave her a saucy wink and picking up her cases as if they weighed nothing, minced exaggeratedly ahead. 'Who you want is Sister Kent, Residency Sister. She'll tell you your room number. Ask her to send for Joe and I'll take these over there.'

'Thank you very much—Joe. How come you're working here?'

'Funny how things work out, isn't it? I had a holiday here, see, come with the blokes from the factory and thought it was grand. When I get back I heard that they was laying off workers. Hadn't had no warning—nothing. But there I was, out of a job. They give me redundancy money, so I packed up and come over here.' He gave a wicked wink. 'Hoped to pick up one of those *señoritas!*'

Hilary laughed. 'And did you?'

'Not so's you'd notice. I 'ad to bring me old woman with me, didn't I?'

'That was tough,' Hilary laughed.

She waited until the sound of his footsteps died away before knocking on the door. A young-looking woman with dark curly hair said, 'How do you do? I'm Sister Kent and you, I suspect, are Nurse Wilson from England. We're expecting you. Do sit down.'

'Thank you.' Hilary took the chair opposite her.

'So, as I like to get these things straight I might as well ask you right away if it was the sun or a young man who enticed you out here.'

Hilary smiled and knew that if she told the truth she would say that both had influenced her. But she shook her head.

'I'd written to a number of hospitals without success—it's rather difficult in England at the moment. Then I saw your advertisement, and as I'd just returned from a holiday here I applied for it. Needless to say I was delighted when I was accepted.'

Sister Kent nodded. 'Quite a coincidence. But you could do worse. I've been over here nearly four years now and I like it as much as I ever did.'

'I can't speak Spanish at all and I've been worried that I might have difficulty with understanding the patients' needs,' Hilary confessed.

'Then stop worrying, because it doesn't matter at all. Most of the staff and the patients are English, so it's no different from an English hospital, except of course that we get the sunshine here. And frankly I can't get too much of that.'

'I think I'll feel the same. So the patients are mostly English? How's that?'

'Oh, a lot of English people live out here now—retired couples and young people unable to get work back home come here to start up a business. Property is a lot less expensive out here, you see,' Sister Kent explained.

'Yes, and of course if they fall ill they like to be in an English-speaking hospital?'

'Yes, it's the language that makes the difference, because there are some excellent Spanish hospitals for those who prefer them.'

'So is this a busy hospital?'

'Goodness, yes. Particularly in Casualty. Situated as we are on the busy road to Malaga, we get our share of RTAs, as you can imagine.'

'And if the casualties are Spanish, do they still come here?' asked Hilary.

'Nurse Wilson, we're a hospital, not a sorting office! Of course they come here.'

Hilary flushed. 'I—I just wondered whether there was a Spanish hospital nearby.'

'There's one not too far away, and if the

patient asks and we think they can be safely moved we'll send them there.'

Sister Kent took a large red-covered book and ran her fingers down a column.

'Here we are. Wilson, Hilary. Staff nurse. Room twenty-four, Block A.'

'Thank you, Sister. I have two heavy cases outside if you——'

'I'll get Joe to take them across for you.' Sister spoke into the phone. 'Now tomorrow morning you'll start off in A and E at seven-fifteen. No doubt you will eventually be moved to another ward, but you'll be there for the time being.'

'Yes, I see. Thank you, Sister.'

'What you want to do is look around the hospital, find out where everywhere is. The staff room you'll see signposted practically everywhere, and when you've unpacked it would be a good idea to go along there and introduce yourself to anyone who's off duty.'

Joe tapped on the door, put his head around and said, 'Right you are, miss. Off we trot.'

Hilary was pleased to discover that she had a room to herself, although it was little more than a cubicle. Catching sight of herself in the mirror, she gave a gasp of dismay. In this wonderful sunshine she looked a complete misfit in her anorak and tweed skirt. Her hair looked a mess and her cherished sun-tan seemed to have vanished completely.

When she had unpacked she showered and

changed into a cotton dress, then decided that instead of going straight to the staff room she would walk down to the sea-front and see again the area which she remembered.

Leaving the hospital grounds, she crossed the busy road, skirted the restaurant where Nick had often taken her, and strolled down the hilly lane that led to the promenade. She stood there in the warm evening looking and listening to the waves that broke against the rocks and the swish as they withdrew. There were plenty of people about, some walking in the sandy cove and others on the cliffs, and although there was the hum of talk and laughter there was still a peaceful atmosphere. Later, she knew, everywhere would become more lively as family parties made their way to the restaurant or down to the promenade. She breathed in the warm sweet air and smiled. It was good here.

But now it was time to get back to the hostel, to meet some other nurses and to get something to eat. Hesitantly she opened the door to the staff room, and saw that it was a modernised version of the one at the Memorial Hospital. The windows had iron grilles and painted shutters in place of curtains and the chairs and tables were of the garden variety which could easily be used out of doors when desired. It looked a summery scene, with nurses in white cotton dresses piped with jade green sitting in groups and chatting together. Hilary felt she couldn't just barge in on any of them, so she sat on a chair near the door feeling lost. After a while a dark-eyed girl noticed her and beckoned to her to join her.

'Hello,' she said, 'I'm Betty Forman, and that's Linda, Jill and Carol. You're new here?'

'Yes, I'm Hilary Wilson, and I've just come from England to work here.'

'And how is old England? I came here from Liverpool over a year ago.'

'England's fine. It was wet and windy when I left,' Hilary laughed.

'You don't get much of that here, but I'm going back in the autumn and looking forward to it,' Betty told her.

'Why? Don't you like it here?'

'Yes, I've enjoyed it a lot, but I like Liverpool, warts and all. Well, it's home, and I'll be going back to my family and my boy-friend. What brings you here?'

'The usual—the sun and the change. No, actually it was because it was so difficult to get a job at home. I tried for lots without any luck.'

'That doesn't sound very promising for me, does it? But I don't really mind. I'll be getting married at Christmas.'

Linda stared at Betty with challenging eyes. 'So what? You don't mean to stop working then, do you?'

'Why not? I'm not one of your Women's Lib lot. I'll do myself a favour and get my husband to keep me in a better style of life than the one I'm accustomed to.' Betty gave Hilary a wink.

'That sounds an excellent idea,' Hilary laughed. 'Tell me, what are the staff like here? Are they easy to get along with?'

A ginger-haired bespectacled girl answered her. 'They vary, the same as in every hospital. Most of them are okay.'

'Apart from Dr Sanders,' said Betty.

'Dr Sanders? I like him,' said Linda.

'So does everybody, but he's a perfectionist, you know he is.'

'I think that's how it should be. Anyhow, he looks so gorgeous he couldn't do anything wrong in my eyes.'

'He couldn't do anything wrong, full stop. But all the same . . . '

They went on arguing amiably, and Hilary realised that she was hungry.

'Where's the canteen? I'm starving,' she said at last.

They all trooped down the corridors to get their supper, which could have been served up at the Memorial Hospital. Hilary pulled a face.

'I expected to get something exotic here in Spain, something with a name I couldn't even pronounce. And what do I get? Stew, diced vegetables and mashed potato! We had that daily back home.'

Betty laughed. 'Don't forget this is an English hospital.'

'You mean it all comes from the same central source?'

'That's right,' Betty joked.

Not wanting to inflict her company on her new companions for the rest of the evening, Hilary left them and went out into the grounds. It was so warm that the slight breeze merely caressed her. Leaning on the gate, she gazed down at the restaurant and wondered whether Nick was in there, and tried to work out why she was slightly reluctant to meet him again. Because he was one of the reasons she had wanted to come here. Yet now she wondered whether he was as good-looking, as charming, such fun to be with as she imagined.

At the time she had believed he was sincere when he suggested she should stay on and work for him, but now she was not so sure. It was probably holiday talk. Other girls would have tumbled to that right away, but she had no experience of holiday friendships either here or in England. Now, away from his compelling personality, common sense told her that such friendships were rootless so probably shortlived. All the same, she wished she had let him know she was coming here, for to see him unexpectedly could be embarrassing, especially if he was with other people. Now she came to think of it, she hadn't been out with him a great deal and had probably read too much in their friendship. She pulled some leaves off a bush. She could either go to the restaurant and risk seeing him with some other girl or spend the rest of the evening in her room. She didn't fancy either very much. Then, with a toss of her head, she crossed the road and made her way to the restaurant.

She was already inside when she realised that 'that man' could well be there, if it was his restaurant. She was on her way to a vacant table when a hand gripped her arm, and she gasped. She might have known, he was going to tell her that she couldn't sit there. With her heart thudding she turned to face him. Instead it was Nick who stood there, looking just as friendly and handsome as she remembered.

'It's little Hilary, by all that's wonderful!' He held her by the shoulders and kissed both her cheeks in the continental way. Then he turned to his two companions whom she remembered seeing in his office last time she was here. 'You remember Hilary?'

'Well, hi. Another holiday already? Some people have all the luck!'

'And not a dicky-bird to me, isn't that great!' Nick's brown eyes looked at her reproachfully.

'Well, it all happened so quickly, I probably got here before a letter would have done. Anyhow, I've only arrived late this afternoon and here I am looking for you because I know you spend ninety per cent of your time here,' Hilary told him with a laugh.

'Ninety per cent of my time?' Nick drew his dark brows into a straight line. 'I assure you that ninety per cent of my time I'm flogging properties, and it's only when I've done a deal that I pop in here for a modest glass of vino to celebrate. Would you deny me that?'

'A-a-ah, poor Nick!' his companions chorused.

He grinned. 'So I'm pleased to know that common sense has prevailed and you've come to work for me. Good, good.'

She shook her head. 'No, I know you don't earn enough to pay my salary as well as for your modest glass of wine, so I'll be working for someone else.'

Nick's eyes narrowed and the laughter faded from them. His voice was ice-cold as he said, 'For another property developer?'

'N—no, of course not,' she said, taken aback by his reaction. 'I—I'm going to work in the hospital across the road.'

His smile returned, and it was like illuminating a dark room. 'Some people are gluttons for punishment!' He turned to the others. 'Would you credit that? I gave her the chance of working for us and she's opted for slogging it out over there. She must be mad!'

'I'm not so sure,' his partner said. 'Maybe she's got her head screwed on the right way.'

'And what sort of a friend do you call yourself?'

Hilary enjoyed listening to their friendly banter and the wine, and felt it had been a delightful evening when on leaving her in the hospital grounds Nick laid his bronzed cheek against her fair hair and murmured,

'Why didn't you come to be with me, honey?'

'Because—because—' she said breathlessly, 'you—you go too quickly for me.'

'Too quickly? Why, what have I done? I've given you all the time in the world to make up your mind. What is it you want?'

'I—I want to look at you and myself from a distance, if you know what I mean. After all, we don't really know one another very well, do we?'

He raised his shoulders and spread his hands. 'But this would be a wonderful chance to get to know each other better.'

'But if I were to leave nursing I would have burnt my boats, and I—I'm not sure that's what I want,' Hilary said thoughtfully.

'So you want me to be patient?'

'Yes, Nick, please.'

'But that isn't my nature, honey.'

She gave a big sigh. 'Well, I—I can't——'

He bent down and placed an audacious kiss on her mouth.

'Okay, honey, I'll work on it.'

'How do you mean?' Hilary looked up at him questioningly.

'Just that I enjoy a challenge,' he said.

Then he was gone, and she watched his lithe figure as he strode away.

She smiled. He was just as attractive as she remembered. It was going to be fun seeing him, and maybe—who could tell as yet? Maybe she would do as he asked. It was an exciting thought.

CHAPTER THREE

ON MONDAY morning Hilary made her way to the Casualty Department to report to Sister Cas. She was a formidable-looking woman, almost of retirement age, with greying hair scraped back into a bun. Her gooseberry-green eyes looked as if they had seen everything and liked nothing and nobody, and at this moment, in particular, Hilary. She stared over her, from the top of her fair hair, down the slim length of her in her white and green seersucker uniform, then up to her round, almost childlike face. Then she gave a smothered snort.

'Hm. So you're Nurse Wilson from England?'

'Yes, Sister,' Hilary said with a smile.

'Denvers—my name is Denvers. Sister Denvers,' she added accusingly.

'Sister Denvers,' Hilary repeated obediently.

'Have you been to Spain before?'

'Yes, I was here on holiday a few weeks ago—Sister Denvers.'

'And I suppose you think this is going to be another holiday?'

Hilary looked at her as if she was hypnotised and shook her head. 'N—n——'

'You're here to work and I'm here to make

sure that you do,' snapped Sister.

Hilary started back as if she had been slapped in the face. 'Of—of course, Sister Denvers.'

'Now just because there are no patients waiting it doesn't mean that you've got nothing to do. Take a look around so that you know where the admission forms, etcetera, are to be found, we don't want to see you wandering around like a lost soul when we're busy. Then sterilise the trolleys and lay them out ready. And——'

Much to Hilary's relief the telephone rang in Sister's office and she trudged along to answer it.

Hilary puffed out her cheeks. It wasn't going to be much fun working under Sister Denvers. During her training when she had worked in various affiliated hospitals she had worked with a variety of Sisters and naturally enough some were not as nice as others, but never had she encountered anyone so blatantly unfriendly as Sister Denvers.

Carol Jenks, who had been preparing a trolley nearby, grinned at her.

'Dear Denvers is up to standard today,' she observed.

'Gosh, is she like that to everybody, or is it just me?' Hilary took a hasty look over her shoulder to make sure she was not overhead.

'She isn't like that to everybody, oh no. To the doctors, unless they're very young, she's all sweetness and charm, intelligence and dedication. It's only if you're young, female and not bad-looking that you're in for it. But take heart, she can't stay here for ever.'

'That's not a lot of comfort at the moment. So where are those wretched admission forms kept?'

'On that shelf outside her office, together with the case sheets and X-ray forms. Everything you need, really, and right under her beady eye.'

'What's the procedure here?' Hilary asked.

'Take the patient's particulars, get them into an examination bay, undress them and buttonhole a doctor.'

Hilary nodded. 'It's the same everywhere, I suppose.'

'And why not? The only difference here is that student nurses are a bit thin on the ground, so there are extra things you'll be expected to do, like helping the dressers, arranging for the mobile X-ray machine to be brought in and finding out where there are any spare beds. Apart from that, being a general dogsbody if Denvers has anything to do with it.'

A couple came into the department, the woman was limping and leaning on the man's arm.

'Shall I see to them?' Hilary asked Carol.

'Sure. Be my guest,' she replied.

Hilary went up to the woman and asked her what had happened.

'It's my ankle, Nurse. There was this boy tearing along on his bike and I thought he was going to knock me down, so I moved away quickly and stepped on a loose stone which turned over. And it's swollen up and very painful.'

'You've probably sprained it, but we'll soon find out. Come into this cubicle.' She took the woman's arm and asked the man to wait outside.

'I hope to goodness it isn't broken, or it will completely spoil our holiday,' the woman said anxiously.

'No, I think you'd be in much more pain if it was broken. But we'll take a picture to make sure. Keep your fingers crossed that it's just a sprain.

While the radiographer was attending to her, Hilary saw an ashen-faced woman crouched on a chair groaning with pain and with her hands pressed against her back. Hilary hurried for a porter to wheel her into a cubicle, believing she could be in labour. Her pain seemed so intense that she either could not or would not answer her questions. So Hilary went to find a doctor, and read his name-plate which said he was Dr Constable.

'I have a patient in great pain, Doctor, could you come, please? I think she's pregnant.'

He gave the woman a cursory examination. 'She isn't pregnant, it's renal colic and possibly stones in the kidney. I'll give her a pain-killer, and we'd better have an X-ray if you'll arrange that.'

'Yes, Doctor.' Hilary prepared the injection

and handed it to the doctor, then rolled up the woman's sleeve.

He leaned forward to give the injection, then started back in horror. 'This woman is a drug addict!' he exclaimed furiously. 'Just look at those prick marks!' He turned away. 'I'll send someone else,' he said, and with a swirl of his jacket he had gone.

Hilary had to attend to a woman who came staggering into the ward reeling as if she had drunk too much. Hilary took her arm and pushed her none too gently on to a chair. Then she hesitated. This woman she thought was drunk had no smell of alcohol on her breath. Hilary touched her cheeks and found they were cold and clammy. She slumped over in the chair.

'Carol, will you come here, please? I need a hand to get this patient into a cubicle.'

Together they lifted her on to the bed and Carol went in search of a doctor. It was Dr Constable again, and he examined the patient swiftly and silently.

'This patient is a diabetic. Prepare twenty grammes of dextrose powder with water, please, Nurse. She'll have to be admitted, so will you see to that.'

Things quietened down after that and Hilary arranged with Carol that she would go for first lunch. She didn't look forward to going to the canteen where she was a stranger. At the Memorial Hospital mealtimes had been the highlights of the day, not for the food, which was abysmal, but for seeing friends and joking and exchanging gossip.

She chose a salad which was nicely prepared and a great improvement on the stew.

'Over here!' a voice called.

She looked around and saw Betty sitting at a table beside the open door and looking out on the garden.

'Hello, nice to see you here—I didn't expect to see anyone I knew. And I hate eating on my own, you've nothing to stop you thinking about the food,' said Hilary.

'I never mind sitting alone, it gives me a chance to think.'

'Well, you've got your wedding to think about, and that must be exciting.'

'That's true. How have you been getting on with old Denvers? I didn't warn you about her, I wanted you to have a night's rest first.'

'She's dreadful, isn't she? I've never met anyone like her before.'

'You'll get used to her,' Betty assured her. 'Have you been busy?'

'In patches.'

'That's always the way. I think they queue up outside until there are a row of them.'

'You'd think so. We had a woman in this morning complaining of pains. I thought she was in labour. Dr Constable thought she had stones in her kidney and got me to prepare a pain-killing injection. He was just going to inject her when he saw that she was a drug addict. He was livid!'

Betty nodded. 'He would be. Oh, it *was* Dr Constable, I suppose?'

'Yes. Why?'

'Well, he lost his son that way.'

'You mean—drugs?'

'Yes. Dr Constable was divorced and had his son living with him, and he got on to drugs when he was at university. He was studying medicine and supposed to be pretty clever. Anyhow, when Dr Constable found out, he did everything in his power to get him off them, but it was no use.'

'That must be awful!' exclaimed Hilary. 'What a waste! No wonder he was so mad at her he wouldn't attend to her. It's funny, I never imagine that doctors have family problems, but of course they're only human beings.'

Betty's eyes twinkled mischievously. 'You'd better not let Dr Sanders hear you say that!'

'Say what?'

'That they're only human beings. He likes to think he's God Almighty.'

Hilary laughed. 'This Dr Sanders sounds quite something. I should imagine he and Sister Denvers would make a good pair.'

Betty threw back her head and laughed. 'Heavens, you won't say that when you see him!'

'Why? Is he old enough to be her father or young enough to be her son?'

'The latter. But that's not the reason.'

'What is, then?'

'You wait and see.'

'Has he got two heads or something?'

'No. More's the pity.'

Betty got up to leave then, and went out of the canteen still laughing.

Hilary went back to the ward early from lunch to give Carol the chance of having a longer one. Standing beside an examination bay was a consultant and a group of doctors, a physiotherapist and Carol. Hilary sidled up to her.

'What's going on?' she asked.

'I'm not sure. Somebody has got something and Mr Flower doesn't know what it is. Let's get closer.'

Hilary looked around to make sure there were no patients waiting and eased her way in the group.

Mr Flower, the consultant, was talking to a man sitting on a bed in the cubicle. Hilary peeped in and saw that he was a healthy-looking man, weatherbeaten rather than sunburnt. He was frowning as he stared at his hand, but when he looked up his eyes looked as if they were more accustomed to laughing.

'So you're on holiday from England?' Mr Flower asked.

'That's right, for a couple of weeks.'

The consultant took the man's hand in his and peered down at two white lumps encircled with a band of colours on his thumb. He touched it gently. 'Is it painful?' he asked.

The man wrinkled his forehead. 'Not terribly. It's beginning to hurt a bit.'

Mr Flower nodded. 'And how long has it been like this?'

The young man thought for a moment. 'The lumps have been there—well, they've been growing for about six weeks. They didn't give any trouble at all. Then this coloured area arrived, the last week or so.'

'Over a week? Did you see your GP about it?'

'Yes, and he didn't have a clue. Suggested I saw the vet.' He chuckled. 'I might say we're all pals, I've know them both for years.'

Mr Flower looked at him coldly, obviously disliking his flippancy.

'So why have you come here today?'

'I didn't much care for the look of it, although I knew it wasn't very serious because I haven't got a red line going up my arm.'

Mr Flower eyed him thoughtfully, then went outside the cubicle followed by his entourage.

'Well, gentlemen, have you any suggestions?'

The Registrar shook his head. 'Can't say I have. I've never seen anything like it before.'

The senior houseman said, 'They look like cysts, but what the coloured area is beats me.'

'I suppose he couldn't be having us on, could he, sir?' the junior houseman asked.

'How do you mean, Jones?'

'Could it be a tattoo or dye put around a

cyst—or something——' His voice faltered and faded away.

Mr Flower shook his head. 'I must confess I'm baffled. I've never even seen anything like it in illustrations.'

A cultured voice said, 'Is this a private party or can anyone join in?'

They turned as one. Hilary's heart felt as if it had been tossed like a pancake. For there was 'that man' himself, white-coated, with a stethoscope hanging from his pocket. So he was a doctor. And here. And it had never occurred to her.

'Ah, Sanders, have you any bright ideas on this? Care to take a look?'

So he was the famous Dr Sanders whom the nurses spoke and joked about. Hilary could see why Betty had laughed when she suggested that he and Sister Denvers should make a twosome. Because he looked even more delectable than ever. The only person who didn't seem impressed by him or particularly pleased to see him was Mr Flower.

Dr Sanders greeted the man with a smile. 'Hello,' he said pleasantly. 'So you've set us a bit of a poser, haven't you? May I take a look-see?'

He held the man's hand in his. The difference in the two was very noticeable, for his was long and narrow and well manicured, whereas the other was strong, capable-looking and gnarled.

'It's a countryman's hand, isn't it?' Dr Sanders remarked with a smile.

'That's right. I farm a few acres in England. I'm lucky to have got away for a short holiday.'

'What have you got? Sheep?'

'Chiefly.'

Dr Sanders was apparently admiring the colours on the man's thumb.

'Quite attractive, isn't it?'

'If you like that sort of thing.'

'How are your sheep doing this year?'

'Pretty well. We've had a dip built recently which will save a lot of hassle. We had a bit of bad luck the other day, though, a prize ram died for no apparent reason. The vet said it was a heart attack. I reckon it must have died from shock when it saw we'd got round to having the dip built at last,' the patient added with a chuckle.

'That's the way it goes, isn't it? It can happen.' Dr Sanders sat on the edge of the bed next to the man and they chatted like old friends. As he spoke he examined the lumps more closely.

'Had you cut it or grazed it at all?' he asked.

The man shook his head. 'Not so's you'd notice.'

'What made you come here today?'

'A bullying wife,' he laughed.

Mr Flower moved impatiently. 'So you've no idea, Sanders?'

His reply was an indifferent glance.

'Tell me,' he said to the patient, 'has there

been an occasion when instead of eating lamb one of the little blighters had a go at you?'

The man grinned and frowned, then clicked his fingers. 'Yes, got it! It was when I was dosing them. As you know, they've got teeth in the front of the jaw and at the back, but there's a space between where you can insert the syringe and dose them. One of them was a bit fractious, I remember now, and as it pulled away his teeth grazed my thumb—it was just about here, too. Did that cause it?'

Dr Sanders stared at him. 'What did you do about it at the time?'

The man looked surprised. 'Carried on dosing them, they were all lined up, so there wasn't anything else I *could* do.'

'No, I understand. Well, you'll be pleased to know that I can tell you what the trouble is.'

The other doctors drew closer.

'Jolly good, let's hear it, then,' the young man said.

'I've got some good news and some bad. Which do you want first?'

'Get the bad bit over and done with,' the man chuckled.

'As you wish.' Hilary's stomach muscles tightened as she saw the smug, pleased-with-himself look on the doctor's face. 'I'm afraid the bad news is that there's no cure for what you've got.'

Alarm sprang up in the young man's face and there was a general movement amongst the doctors. Mr Flower looked angrily at Dr Sanders, as if he disapproved of such a callous way of imparting bad news.

'You're kidding,' the young man said.

Dr Sanders smilingly shook his head. 'I'm not. But the good news is that there's no cause for alarm, because your body's own antibodies are dealing with it satisfactorily. It will gradually clear up of its own accord and you won't need any treatment.

'How long will it take?'

'A few more weeks.'

Mr Flower looked at him coldly. 'Your diagnosis, please.'

Dr Sanders crossed his long legs and leaned back. 'Certainly. This patient has Orf, which you get from sheep. Looking at it through a microscope you'll see that the virus has serrated edges, which means that it's being dealt with by the body's own resources.'

Mr Flower nodded. 'I see. So you've come across this condition before?'

'Yes. I had a spell in Australia before I came here, and Orf is not uncommon amongst the sheep farmers. It looks worse than it is.'

'Thank you, Sanders, that's most interesting and informative.' He turned to his companions. 'You'll keep notes on this, of course.'

Hilary watched with mixed feelings. A part of her felt inordinately proud that Dr Sanders had been able to diagnose the problem, but another part of her felt rebellious. Why couldn't he be proved wrong, just once in a while?

He and Mr Flower exchanged a few words, then Mr Flower walked away. Dr Sanders was making his way to Sister Denvers' office when he saw Hilary and stopped. Her body felt awash with heat as his eyes travelled slowly over her. In his blue, thickly-lashed eyes there was a gleam of recognition.

'I know your face, but I don't think I've seen you in this hospital before, have I?' he asked, almost accusingly.

Oh God! He was going to remember her rude reply to him which she so bitterly regretted.

'I've only just started working here, Doctor,' she said, hoping the conversation would end there.

But he was having none of that. 'And when I saw you . . . ' He frowned and clicked his fingers. 'It was on the beach, I believe?'

Hilary bit her lip. 'I—I was on holiday then.'

'Ah, a lady of leisure—one quite possibly *not* accustomed to the climate, huh?'

Hilary looked down at the floor, unwilling to meet his teasing eyes. So he remembered everything she had said.

'This time I suggest you take my advice and don't try too hard to get a sun-tan. It would be a shame to ruin that delicate complexion.'

She flicked him a glance—then wished she hadn't for he was looking amused and she felt herself dwindling in size.

Sister Denvers bustled up, her face beaming.

'That was brilliant of you, Dr Sanders. Whatever would they have done if you hadn't been here?'

He laughed. 'Probably nothing. And that would have made no difference.'

'Well, even at my age I've learnt something today,' Sister Denvers said, and if she had been a younger woman Hilary would have sworn she was making eyes at him.

She suddenly turned and saw Hilary. 'Nurse Wilson! In this hospital I do not tolerate staff standing and staring. Will you get on, please.'

'Yes, Sister Denvers.'

Hilary walked away, but glanced back over her shoulder. He looked if possible even more sexy and attractive in his white jacket with its torn pocket than he did without it.

For a moment she forgot where she was and felt bemused. Then she blinked and shook her head and went to attend to a waiting patient.

CHAPTER FOUR

It was seven o'clock and Hilary was getting ready to meet Nick. Here in Spain the next few hours would be the most social of the day, and that was a novelty to her. She brushed her fair hair until it shone like gold, looked at her pink and white skin and hoped it would soon be suntanned. She thought of 'that man's' second warning. Fancy him being a doctor and in this very hospital! She wondered if she would have applied to come here had she known. And drat the man, of course she would, because it gave her a thrill just to see him. There was something so self-contained about him, as if his immaculate, good-looking exterior was a cover for all kinds of emotions which only someone who knew him very intimately would know. He was supremely self-confident and didn't care a fig for Mr Flower's opinion, that was obvious. Hilary wondered who was the senior of the two and guessed that although it would matter a great deal to Mr Flower, to Dr Sanders it would be completely unimportant. So he remembered her! Her wide blue eyes stared at her reflection beseechingly. She hoped it was not because of her rude retort. Why had he looked amused?

Had he by some devilish insight known that her nose had actually peeled? She wouldn't put it past him. She could well imagine how pleased he would now be feeling to have been able to diagnose Orf when nobody else had heard of it.

Heavens, it was time to meet Nick. She gave herself a final hasty glance, picked up her handbag and hurried out through the grounds. When she drew near the restaurant she could see that he had not yet arrived. He had told her to go in and order a drink if she got there first, but she decided she would rather wait and watch the people making their way to the sea-front. Gradually the lights sprang up everywhere and from the restaurant came the sound of music and talk and laughter. But still Nick did not arrive. Eventually Hilary decided to do as he said and go in and get herself a drink, although she didn't fancy sitting alone.

She sat at a table near the door and ordered a glass of wine. Time dragged. She looked at her watch and saw that it had gone eight, and doubted whether Nick would come now. The door beside her opened and closed frequently as people came and went, and every time she looked up expectantly. And then—everthing inside her curled up in embarrassment, for who should come in but Dr Sanders. She knew now, of course, that he was not the owner of the restaurant, but goodness! he looked the part. It wasn't that he was so much taller than anyone else, he just gave that impression, he stood so upright with his handsome head in the air and looked down his nose as if he was in charge of everything and everyone. She lowered her head and cringed, hoping to make herself invisible, but she just had to look up again. Then she saw that he was not alone, and she felt a strange feeling of loss. His arm was laid casually around a girl's shoulders as they hesitated, looking for a vacant table.

Hilary took in her appearance with a glance —quite tall, well built, pale complexion and glossy dark hair which hung to just below her ears and ended with a curve on each cheek. She looked as if she could have once been a school games captain and was now, probably, a physiotherapist. She was not particularly pretty or feminine, but she was apparently the type of girl Dr Sanders admired. Was she his wife or fiancée?

She was so engrossed in staring at this girl and wondering about her that she gave a start of surprise when Dr Sanders said in his unmistakable voice,

'Good evening.'

She felt her face flush as she looked up, but she need not have bothered, for they were already walking away to a table further down the room.

And still Nick hadn't arrived. Hilary had no intention of staying here feeling abandoned, knowing that at any moment Dr Sanders might notice her solitariness. She wouldn't put it past him for him to come across and tell her that she shouldn't be sitting there alone, that it wasn't the thing for a young lady to do. She drained her glass and left. The evening had been a complete disaster.

And what did Nick think he was playing at? He had said he would meet her at seven-fifteen. She couldn't blame him for being a few minutes late, he could easily be held up, but it was now half past eight. That settled it; she was not going to arrange to meet him again. If they met by chance then she might agree to have a drink with him, but that was all. So Dr Sanders was either married or engaged, which was the most natural thing in the world, yet she had never given it a thought. Suddenly Spain didn't seem so nice, and she wished she was back home amongst her friends and family. And it could rain all it liked!

She waited for the traffic, then crossed the road. She was just turning into the drive when she heard running footsteps behind her. With a leap of her heart she clutched her handbag and swung round. It was Nick, with a radiant smile on his face.

'Why are you walking in the wrong direction, honey?' he asked, putting his hands on her shoulders.

With a surge of anger intensified by shock Hilary glared up at him.

'Because I'd waited for you far too long. Do

you know what time it is? I've been waiting over an hour!'

'Never mind, sweetie, here I am, better late than never. And I've done a deal which, if it goes through, will bring me in a couple of grand. Let's celebrate.'

'No, I'm going back now.'

'Oh no, you're not.' With his arm encircling her waist Nick ran her across the road and down the hill to the restaurant so that her feet scarcely touched the ground. She was breathless and laughing when they reached there, and she saw no point in spoiling what was left of the evening by being angry.

As it was fairly late the restaurant was full, and they wandered up and down looking for somewhere to sit. Hilary saw from the corner of her eye that Dr Sanders and his lady were on the point of leaving, and she turned the other way, hoping not to be seen. But Dr Sanders, who missed nothing, said,

'Hello, again. If you're looking for a table take ours, we're just about to leave.'

Hilary gave a faint smile and thanked him, but Nick held out his hand.

'Well, hello, that's good of you. I see you know Hilary. I'm Nick Trowbridge, the estate agent—you've probably heard of me. And you are—?'

'Sanders—Dr Steve Sanders. And Miss Wendy Smith.'

Hilary saw that at close quarters she looked

very aristocratic. Smith? She bet it was spelt with a y and an e. Then it dawned on her: if that was her name shc couldn't be his wife. Nick was chatting away to him as if they were old friends, but at last the couple left and she and Nick took their places.

'So he's a doctor at your hospital, eh? You'd have thought they'd cook up a better name than Smith, wouldn't you?'

'I don't know what you're talking about. I don't know anything about either of them, and I shouldn't have dreamed of stopping to speak to them,' Hilary said shortly.

Nick's eyes were two laughing slits. 'You're no businesswoman! I speak to anybody who might conceivably have a few pesetas to spend. That way you become acquainted, and if they or their friends are thinking of buying property who better to approach than someone they know and can trust?'

'Knowing you wouldn't mean they could trust you. Quite the opposite, I should have thought,' Hilary teased, half seriously.

His eyes opened wide and he looked quite hurt. 'But I'm an honest man, I promise you I am.'

'You haven't apologised for being late yet,' she reminded him, still remembering the long wait.

'I know what it is, honey, you want something to eat.' He clicked his fingers to attract the waiter's attention.

Hilary decided not to keep on about it but to change the subject.

'I'll tell you something about Dr Sanders,' she said. 'In Casualty today a man came in with two lumps on his thumb and with a circle of colours around them. None of the other doctors had a clue what it was, but he was able to tell them it was something called Orf. I bet you don't know what that is.'

Nick made no reply, and when she glanced at him she realised he hadn't listened to a word she'd said.

'Nick!'

His wandering eyes came back to settle on her.

'Yes, honey?'

'You weren't listening to me.'

'Surely I was,' he protested.

'What did I say, then?'

The waiter arrived and Nick asked for a menu. 'What would you like?' he asked.

Hilary shrugged, feeling she had been ignored all evening. But she wanted to eat.

'I'll have the tunnyfish salad, please,' she said.

'And the same for me,' said Nick.

When the waiter had gone she said, 'What was it I said, then?'

He threw up his hands with a laugh. 'Now she asks me! Honey, all day long I'm inundated with people talking. Can I remember what each of them say?'

'Oh, Nick, you could wriggle out of any

awkward situation, I do believe!'

With a mischievous grin he looked into her eyes and said, 'I love you.'

He gave a friendly wave to two women sitting at a nearby table. 'I'm hoping to sell them an apartment,' he explained. 'They're teachers who've taken early retirement. One of them is keen, the other is dragging her heels—the usual pattern.'

'Why is she hesitating?'

Nick's eyebrows shot up. 'Does she really want to leave England; would they be able to manage on their pensions; is the apartment a good investment or would they do better to buy a bungalow on the south coast of England? As soon as you set her mind at rest over those points she comes up with another list as long as your arm.'

'Well, I suppose it's a big step for them to take. And what she's no doubt really worried about is whether they'll get on well together when neither is working. They'd be with each other all the time, wouldn't they?'

Nick laughed. 'Come on, we'll have a word with them. At least our salads won't get cold!'

The two ladies welcomed him with a smile.

'Well, how nice to see you both here enjoying yourselves. Miss Quick, Miss Bell, I'd like you to meet Miss Wilson who's recently come out here from England to live.'

The ladies looked at Hilary with interest. 'Oh, really?'

'Yes indeed,' Nick continued quickly. 'After coming here on holiday she liked it so much she decided to settle here. And she hasn't regretted it for a moment. Have you?' He turned briefly to Hilary, then went on, 'Now do let me get you a drink.' He glanced at what they had in their glasses. 'Is it the same again?'

'Thank you, yes. That's very kind of you,' they said.

After he had given the order he said, 'Have you heard what the weather's like back in England?'

They shook their heads. 'No?'

'Wet and windy, and gale force winds, I believe. My word, aren't we lucky to be here in the lovely warmth and sunshine! Do you know something? As long as I stay here I'll never grow old.'

Miss Bell eyed Hilary questioningly. 'So you're happy to be living here?'

Hilary swallowed. 'Oh yes—very.'

'And do you miss your friends and relations over there?'

'N—no, I can't say I do. Not yet,' Hilary admitted.

Miss Bell dabbed her mouth with a handkerchief. 'Might I ask you—it's quite a liberty, but I'm rather concerned—how are you finding things financially, compared with living in England?'

Nick leaned both hands on the table. 'Miss Wilson is very comfortable, she took my advice over money matters, you see. After all, it's part of my job to make sure that my clients are satisfied. I mean to say, what good would it do me if I were to try and sell you a property which I knew you couldn't comfortably afford? I'd have you breathing fire and brimstone down my neck, wouldn't I? No, it's in my own interests that the people I sell to don't have to go round with begging bowls, isn't it?' He chuckled.

'Yes, I suppose it is,' Miss Bell laughed.

'That's what I've been telling you, Mary,' said Miss Quick. 'So how about it? We'll have to make up our minds. Well, mine is made up already?'

Miss Bell took off her glasses and polished them. 'Well, Miss Wilson seems to be happy here. It's good to have heard it from the horse's mouth, so to speak. So very well—yes, Mr Trowbridge, yes, I agree.'

Nick laid his hand comfortingly on her shoulder. 'No, please, Miss Bell—I don't want you to agree to something you might regret. Sleep on it, for all our sakes. You see, I don't want you merely to agree, I want you to be as enthusiastic over it as I feel and as Miss Quick is. It's such a charming apartment—and you've seen the marvellous view—and I don't need to tell you its a knock-down price. But I want you to really want it. So shall we leave it at that for the time being, just until you're quite, quite sure?' He gave a winning smile which abruptly faded. ‘Oh dear, there is just one thing. I know it sounds corny, but there really is another couple very keen on buying it. To be fair to everybody—and that’s how I run my business—I won’t be able to hold on to it if they give me a firm offer, much as I’d like to. You do understand, don’t you?’ He looked so abjectly sorry about it that Hilary felt an urge to reassure him.

‘Oh dear!’ Miss Bell looked from Nick to her friend, then back again. ‘Oh well, that settles it, I suppose. We’d better take it,’ she said reluctantly.

Miss Quick looked relieved. ‘That’s excellent, Mary, now we can get on. Will you make out the cheque for the deposit for Mr Trowbridge?’

‘Yes, of course.’ Miss Bell rummaged around in her capacious bag for her cheque book.

‘Oh, there’s no hurry for that,’ said Nick, taking a calculator from his pocket to work out the amount due.

‘Yes, I’ll do it now. How much shall I make it out for?’

‘Well, if you insist,’ he said, telling her the amount. ‘And thank you very much.’

He put it away in his wallet. ‘So if you’ll call in at the office in the morning we can get things started. What time would suit you? Ten-thirty? That’s fine. Incidentally, if you need any advice over the best place to buy curtains or furnishings ask Sarah, the young lady in my office, she’ll be only too pleased to help.’

‘Thank you, Mr Trowbridge, that’s really

very kind of you, and thoughtful too.'

He shook hands with both of them. 'Not at all, it's all part of the service. I want everybody who deals with me to be happy.'

They looked at him fondly. 'It's really been a pleasure doing business with you, Mr Trowbridge. Nobody could have been more helpful.'

'The pleasure is mine. I do my best for all my clients, but there are some, like your good selves, you care about more than others. I'm really glad you've decided to buy that apartment, I feel it's so right for you, so suitable. It's charming and elegant.'

'I feel quite excited,' Miss Quick confessed. 'I know we've done the right thing, Mary.'

'Then we'll leave you to talk about it. Be seeing you,' Nick smiled.

By the time they got back to their table Hilary felt exhausted. 'Gosh! All that effort to sell an apartment!' she exclaimed.

Nick looked triumphant. 'That's the way to do it.'

'That's all very well, but you led them to believe I'd bought a property from you. You used me!'

He raised his shoulders and spread his hands. 'So you've earned your supper, haven't you?'

'But was someone else really after it?' asked Hilary with a frown.

'Most probably,' Nick smiled.

'But did you mean what you said about them doing the right thing?'

He smiled wickedly through half-closed eyes. 'Sure. They'll be happy enough in that block, there's a load of geriatrics there already.'

She looked aghast. 'What a horrible thing to say!' Then, seeing him laughing as if he was thoroughly enjoying himself, she asked doubtfully, 'Are you teasing me?'

'Maybe.' He grinned devilishly. 'We'll drink to that. Do you know something?' She shook her head. 'I like seeing you look worried!'

Whether it was the music or the wine or Nick's lively personality, Hilary's earlier depression vanished and she was soon laughing and talking and feeling this was the pleasantest evening of her life.

With his arm encircling her waist they walked down to the sea-front and along the promenade to the marina with its many sailing boats before returning to the hospital, although it was late. There they stood in the shadow of some bushes and he held her close. With his face next to hers she felt happy and relaxed and began to feel that normally she was too serious and boring. This was how she should be, like Nick, able to laugh and have fun and enjoy the good things of life that money could buy.

'Darling Nick,' she said, and kissed him.

He patted her cheek. 'Sweet dreams, honey,' he said, and started to walk away.

'When will I see you again?' she asked anxiously, as he had not mentioned it.

She saw his teeth gleaming white. 'Every day,

if you come to work for me.'

'No, seriously, Nick. When?'

'Next time they let you out of this prison,' he said, nodding towards the hospital.

'That—that's Saturday.'

'Saturday it is, then.'

'At—at seven?'

'At seven.'

'Oh,' she said, suddenly remembering, 'I finish at four on Saturday.'

'Okay. At four, then,' smiled Nick.

'Wh—where?'

'Where you like.'

'Here?'

'Okay.'

'At four?'

He took her face between his hands and kissed her full on the mouth. 'Sure,' he said.

Then, with a series of leaps and bounds, he disappeared from her view.

When Hilary reached her room she sat on the edge of the bed, her feelings in a turmoil. Nick was so fascinating, so charming, so handsome, that she felt she could be happy for ever just looking at him. And yet there was something so elusive about him. Was he ruthless? Or was he kind? Was he serious in what he said and did or was he joking most of the time? Could she, in fact, rely on him meeting her here on Saturday? She had no reason to doubt him, but his replies had been so facile, so lacking in conviction, that she couldn't feel sure.

She shouldn't have asked when she would see him again, she should have left that to him, that was what a girl was supposed to do. But she had no previous experience of dealing with boy-friends. Boy-friends? But he wasn't that, was he? But if she went to work for him he would be, wouldn't he?

CHAPTER FIVE

EVERYBODY at the hospital was on the alert after a warning was received that there had been a pile-up on the road to Malaga involving a coach and two private cars. Very soon the forecourt was filled with ambulances and the sound of activity as their doors were opened and steps lowered and instructions given as to how the patients should be moved.

Nurses headed by Sister Denvers hurried forward to assist as patients were brought in on stretchers or in wheelchairs. Hilary felt the wave of misery she usually experienced on seeing victims of accidents, for to her they seemed an unnecessary form of suffering. She knew, however, that injuries which looked horrific were frequently not so bad when the wounds and lacerations had been cleaned of blood and grime.

Extra nurses and doctors had been brought in and stretcher cases were lined up in the corridor until the examination bays were free. Emergencies such as this brought out the best in everybody. When help was needed it was given eagerly by anyone who was available and in the wards, wherever there was a space, beds were set up and prepared for admissions. Coffee breaks and off-duty times were not even thought about.

Sister Denvers stopped beside a stretcher and Hilary, nearby, saw her whole demeanour change. Her eyes lost their hardness and sank back in her head and her mouth puckered into a hundred small tucks. On seeing Hilary she said in a voice so gentle and concerned that it was almost unrecognisable,

'Theatre two will need to be prepared, and I want you to assist as required.'

Hilary looked at her questioningly. Sister Denvers jerked her head in the direction of the stretcher.

'It's a child. I'll get Dr Sanders.'

Even after the little girl had been cleaned up and prepared for surgery her injuries looked heartbreakingly severe. When Dr Sanders arrived he gave Hilary no sign of recognition as she tied his gown and he pulled on his cap and mask. On seeing the patient he took a short, sharp breath and his eyes became dark with anguish.

The Registrar and houseman were waiting to assist and Hilary was ready with the sterilised instruments. The anaesthetist adjusted his machine to his satisfaction, then gave a brief nod. Hilary glanced up at Dr Sanders, who stood quite still for several moments with his eyes closed as if in prayer. Then the long and painstaking work began.

During routine operations the surgeon and

his team would frequently chat amongst themselves about matters unconnected with what they were doing. But now the only sounds were the clink of instruments, an occasional request for one, the hiss of the machine and heavy breathing. As the hours passed the heat became unbearable, but Steve Sanders never paused except to glance periodically at the anaesthetist to make sure that all was well at his end and to have his forehead wiped. The other doctors eased their necks and flexed their muscles, but Hilary had got past noticing the ache in her head and back, she was so engrossed in watching Steve's delicate, skilful movements.

At long last he straightened up, nodded, and spoke for the first time.

'We've done what we can. Now it's up to the Almighty.'

Hilary brushed tears from her eyes before anyone should notice them, although she believed they were all concerned with controlling their own emotions.

When she returned from wheeling the child to the recovery room prior to going into intensive care the theatre had emptied, with the exception of Steve Sanders, who was standing as still as a statue. Hilary went up to him and untied his gown and threw it aside. When he automatically peeled off his cap and mask she saw the pallor and lines of utter fatigue etched on his face.

'I'll get you some coffee, sir. Or would you

prefer something stronger?' she asked.

He blinked as if to shake away his thoughts. 'Mm?' he queried.

'Some coffee, sir?'

'Oh, thanks, Nurse.'

She brought him some sandwiches too, guessing rightly that he would not want to sit with the other doctors who might possibly discuss the case. He sank down on a chair in the changing room and drank thirstily. Only then did he seem to come out of a daze and look at Hilary as if seeing her for the first time.

'You must have some coffee too, and there are more sandwiches than I can eat,' he told her.

They sat together in silence. Hilary would have liked to have known what he thought of the little girl's chances, but knew he would not tell her in so many words. Only by the look in his expressive eyes which seemed to have absorbed all the sorrow and suffering in the world would she have been able to guess, but she knew he would rather she didn't ask.

'What time is it, Nurse?'

She glanced at the fob watch on her bodice. 'It's a quarter past three, sir.'

He ran his knuckles across his eyes. 'I want to get away from here for some fresh air—it's stifling! I think I'll drive up into the hills, it should be better there.' As an afterthought he asked if she would like to go too.

Would she! 'Oh yes, that would be lovely,'

she said. Then she remembered that she was still on duty. 'Oh, I don't finish until four o'clock,' she added disappointedly.

'Don't worry about that, I'll have a word. The rush is over now. I'll take a shower and get changed and see you in the car park in twenty minutes or so.'

As Hilary washed and changed she didn't flatter herself that he had invited her to accompany him because it was her company that he desired, she realised that it was a polite invitation he would have extended to anyone who had happened to be there when he voiced his intention. But no matter. She still felt as pleased as a child when it is given an unexpected present. She made up her mind to be as unobtrusive as possible because he would surely need peace as well as fresh air.

They arrived in the car park at the same time. Steve greeted her with a nod and opened the car door. She thanked him and fastened her seat belt, and felt a thrill of satisfaction as he got in beside her. She could see the light brown hairs on his wrist and the slim gold watch as he put his hands on the steering wheel. She pretended to look out of his window, but in reality she was noticing the blue glint of his eyes between his thick curling lashes, his crisp white shirt, beige slacks and soft leather shoes.

They drove in silence off the main road and on to a narrower winding road which led up through the hills. Hilary's muscles tensed as she saw the sheer drop to the right of them, but Steve drove carefully. She gave a shudder as she pictured what the same journey would be like with Nick at the wheel, talking and laughing and looking wickedly happy if she showed any signs of fear.

Nevertheless she was not sorry when Steve drove into a clearing at the side of a safe piece of road and suggested that they sat out for a while. He reached into the boot of his car and took out some rugs and cushions and threw them on the ground.

'This scrub gets so hot from the sun it could burn you,' he explained. 'You'd better sit in the shade of those bushes.'

She took a rug and a cushion and found a sheltered spot.

'Heavens!' she exclaimed, as she touched the ground with her hand. 'Yes, it could give anyone a nasty burn. I wonder it doesn't catch on fire.'

Steve lay, his arms laced behind his head, under an overhanging tree. 'It does, quite frequently.'

They were silent, and although the sun was hot there was cooler air to breathe and it was peaceful after the hectic day.

After a while Steve said drowsily, 'I once saw an amazing sight. I was driving along this road when I saw what looked like a cross of fire ahead of me.'

'Good gracious, what was it?'

'I stopped the car and just stared at it—I

couldn't believe my eyes. Then I decided there must be a logical explanation, so I drove nearer, and gradually I saw that it was a length of scrub that had ignited and exactly at the centre was a slender tree which was also alight. So that was what it was, a burning cross.'

'If it had been Good Friday it would have seemed like an omen of something or other, wouldn't it? It must have looked most impressive.'

He lay back with his eyes closed. 'Are you superstitious?'

'In some ways. I always say "Good morrow, Mick," if I see just one magpie.' Hilary laughed. 'I've even been known to apologise to one if I happen to have overlooked it the first time.'

'Why do you do that? What's with a magpie?'

'The saying is "one for sorrow". Saying "Good morrow" is like crossing your fingers.'

'You cross your fingers if you tell lies. Do you do that?'

She laughed. 'I'd like to be able to say that like George Washington I cannot tell a lie, but of course I do. Cross my fingers, I mean. Do you?'

After a few minutes he said, 'As a medical man I shouldn't be superstitious.'

'I know that. But are you?'

His mouth curved into a smile. 'As a very young child I believed in Santa Claus. But that belief came to a sticky end when my father died.'

'I pretended to believe long after I discovered my presents hidden in a drawer. I remember reading an annual through from cover to cover and then having to pretend it was all new to me on Christmas Day.'

The sun was very hot and Hilary felt her arm burning. She rubbed it and moved it into the shade.

'I'll no doubt get skin cancer in that arm,' she said, without actually thinking—then could have bitten out her tongue.

Steve half opened his eyes, squinting in the sunlight. 'You didn't like being told, did you?'

'We-ell, it was the way you said it,' she told him.

'The way I said it? I can't think of many different ways of making that statement.'

'You sounded bossy.'

'I think perhaps you don't like being told not to do a thing, even if it's for your good,' Steve observed.

Hilary would have argued, but it was too hot and she felt sure he was too tired, so they lay there and watched the planes making their way to and from the airport like large birds in flight and listening to the drone of flies and bees as they hovered around them.

Hilary awoke with a start, wondering momentarily where she was. Then she sat up and looked across at Steve, who was still sleeping. He seemed younger in repose, the square line of his jaw was softened, his lashes cast shadows on his olive-coloured cheek. This sleep would do him good.

It was quite a while later that he stirred, opened his eyes and sat up in one movement. He blinked several times, looked at Hilary and then at his watch.

'Ten past six. Would that be a.m. or p.m.?'

'A.m.,' she chuckled, teasing him. 'We've been here all night and our reputations are in shreds!'

'You can't scare me that easily, I can tell by the position of the sun that it's p.m., and I'm thankful that tomorrow is Sunday and apart from being on call I'm free.'

'Heavens!' She looked at her watch to check the time. Yes, it was gone six, and she had arranged to meet Nick at four o'clock. She felt horribly guilty, especially after the fuss she had made the other night when he had kept her waiting, but there was nothing she could do about it now, so there was no use worrying.

Steve raised his eyebrows. 'What's the trouble?'

Hilary shook her head. 'Oh—nothing. I was just surprised to realise how the time had flown.'

He nodded. 'That's what happens when you fall asleep, it's a waste of time. Shall we get something to eat? There's a small restaurant near here which is quite good.'

'Thank you, that would be nice.'

It was a pleasant restaurant, well patronised and surrounded by tables shaded with umbrellas.

'I can recommend their speciality, it's stuffed

onions,' said Steve. 'Would you care to try them?'

Hilary wrinkled her nose. 'They don't sound very exciting.'

'They are, though. They're very mild and tender and the meat sauce is flavoured with delicious spices that I've never come across anywhere else. But please yourself, of course.'

He handed her the menu, but she saw nothing to take her fancy.

'Okay, I'll try them,' she said without much enthusiasm.

He smiled. 'You could enjoy them, you know, if you didn't object so strenuously to taking my advice.'

They wouldn't dare to be anything other than good, Hilary thought mutinously, but she just flicked him a glance and said nothing.

With crusty buttered bread, fresh fruit and wine it was a meal which could not have been bettered, and the onions were out of this world, Hilary decided. Or maybe it was because she had hardly eaten anything all day.

The air was definitely fresh now, the music was gentle and sweet and the customers were all well behaved. She felt she could have sat here for ever.

'What part of England do you come from, Hilary?'

She had a momentary picture of the little cottage which seemed so far away, so shabby compared with the apartments and expensive homes in Finola.

'In north London,' she replied.

'Ah, as I thought, a typical suburban young lady,' Steve said with a smile which she resented.

This time he was not going to get away with it. If it was the last thing she did she was going to put him in the wrong.

'Probably not as you imagine it,' she said sweetly. 'Actually we've got several acres and a lake.' She warmed to the idea. 'You can't imagine the fun my sister and I had boating and mucking around when we were kids!'

She crossed her fingers as she spoke, then hastily uncrossed them in case he should notice and wonder. Because of course she had lied about the lake, because that was only for the use of the people who lived in the big houses that backed on it. When they were young she and Tessa had indeed spent happy days there, taking it in turn to think up the lovely things that would happen if you lived in one of them.

'We'd have Christmas trees all lit up indoors and in the garden, so that they were reflected in the lake.'

'We'd have parties, and lots and lots of children would come and bring presents wrapped up in fancy paper.'

'On Sundays we'd go riding and wear proper riding clothes, jodhpurs and hard hats.'

'We'd go to dancing classes and wear tutus and ballet shoes.'

'And our mother would take us there in a car.'

It was not that they were jealous or even envious, it was a happy game of makebelieve, after seeing how the other children lived. Sometimes, indeed, they would play a different version of the game, when gypsies camped on the nearby green, and they would pretend that they only had potato sacks for dresses, which they would dye blue and use a piece of string for a belt.

'You're very fortunate to live there, you and your sister must have had an enviable life.' Steve sounded almost wistful.

'Yes, we did. And what part of England are you from?'

'Oxford.' He was silent for a moment, then he said thoughtfully, 'My father died when I was a child and my mother and I became very close. Then she remarried and I was sent to boarding school.'

'That sounds sad,' Hilary said softly.

'Mm. Quite possibly I would have gone there anyway, but at the time I felt unwanted as if I'd been sent there to get me out of the way.'

'And when you left?'

'Oh, they'd had a daughter by then and gone to live in America. I went to university and then to Barts. I spent my vacations with an uncle who was a nice old chap. His wife, unfortunately, rather resented me.'

'What a sad life you've had,' said Hilary,

yearning to take him in her arms and comfort him.

He gave a short laugh. 'Averagc, I should think. Anyhow, it taught me to stand on my own and not to rely on other people.'

'So when you left Barts you went to Australia?'

'Not immediately. But I did spend a couple of years there and now I've had a couple here.'

'And next? Will you settle in England?'

He shrugged. 'I doubt it. I'll probably be on the move again. What about you, how long are you here for?'

'For no specific time,' Hilary told him. 'I just applied for this job and got it. I'd just returned from being on holiday here, you see.'

His beautiful blue eyes looked at her caressingly. 'And you wanted to come back to be with that handsome fellow you were with the other night. Is that it?'

Hilary felt the colour flood her cheeks. 'Well, I—saw the advertisement and——'

His eyes were full of understanding. 'And it seemed too good to be true. I know.' He glanced at his watch. 'Come along, it's time we were getting back.'

The moon had risen now and lights were twinkling from buildings between the olive trees with their grey-green foliage, and from cars as they sped along the road from Malaga. They didn't speak, they just enjoyed the peace and the beauty of their surroundings.

All too soon Hilary saw the hospital ahead and knew that this outing which she had so enjoyed was over. Steve drew the car to a halt to allow her to get out.

'Thank you so much for taking me with you, I've enjoyed it immensely,' she said.

He looked at her with veiled eyes. 'I've enjoyed it too. I needed to be with somebody, and I'm grateful for your company. Thank you.'

He drove off then to the car park. So he had needed to be with someone, almost anyone would have done, she knew that. So why did she feel so sad? She stood there, leaning on the gate, unwilling to go indoors yet, and still thinking over their conversation.

Across the road groups of people were going into the brightly lit restaurant. At the sight of it she remembered that she should have met Nick, and felt guilty. It was going to be hard to explain to him why she hadn't kept the appointment. Should she go across and see if he was there? As she was debating that she saw him come out of the door with a group of friends. He glanced across and saw her standing there, then ran across the road to join her.

He looked angry and huge as he pinned her against the gate with his arms.

'What sort of a game do you think you're playing?' he demanded.

Steve, returning from the car park, paused when he saw them there standing like lovers about to embrace. He watched them for a minute or two, then he turned and walked to his flat in the hospital.

CHAPTER SIX

SEEING that all was quiet in Casualty, Hilary slipped along the corridor to the staff room for a quick cup of coffee. She saw Carol and Betty were already there, so she went to join them.

'I'm going to miss this glorious weather if I go back to England,' Hilary said.

Carol laughed and stretched. 'This afternoon, God willing, I shall be free.'

'*God* willing? You mean Sister Denvers willing, don't you? Or am I confusing the two?' asked Hilary. 'But hold on—I thought you were on duty?'

'I should be, that's true. But I'm taking the afternoon off.'

'Taking it off? What for?'

'It doesn't sound as if she's going to a funeral, so it must be a wedding or a christening,' said Betty uninterestedly as she scanned the pages of an English newspaper.

'If you can be a bit more sociable and drag yourself away from that week-old rag, which, let me remind you, is mine, I'll tell you.'

'Go on, then,' murmured Betty, laughing at a cartoon.

Carol made a grab for the paper and Betty

looked up with bemused eyes.

'What's up?'

'I'm talking to you.'

'What about?'

'Me.'

'That's bound to be riveting. Go on, then.'

'Well now. The beach has never looked more inviting—I know, because I looked at it out of a top-floor window. I'm owed a half-day because I stayed on for an emergency and I feel I shall go crazy if I can't lie in the sun for a few hours. So—I'm taking the afternoon off.'

Betty gave a hoot of laughter. 'I see. So you went up to Denvers and told her that and she said "Quite right, Nurse Jenks, of course you must lie in the sun while we slave away indoors." I can just hear her saying it!'

Carol's eyes danced. 'I'm not daft, I know the odds. I told her that I had raging toothache and the only time my dentist could fit me in was this afternoon. But as it takes ages to get there and back it means the whole afternoon off, doesn't it? Mind you, I had a devil of a job to get out of seeing old Jaws, I had to spin a yarn about needing a special filling.'

'Jaws?' Hilary smiled.

'That's the resident dentist, sometimes known as the fiend of Finola.'

They laughed, but Hilary said, 'I should be afraid I was tempting fate and that I *would* get toothache if I did what you did.'

'Ah, but I'm an accomplished liar, and the devil looks after his own.'

Having drunk her coffee, Hilary hurried back to the ward, leaving the other two laughing and joking.

Although she would not have done what Carol had she was amused and could sympathise with her for wanting to be out in the sunshine. She herself was looking forward immensely to her afternoon with Nick. After his initial anger with her for breaking her appointment with him on Saturday he had become loving and forgiving, showing her a side of his character that surprised her. She wondered where he would take her today, but knew with a light heart that it would be somewhere enjoyable. She could hardly wait.

Although she had only spent a few minutes in the staff room Sister Denvers had noticed her absence.

'Wilson, you're supposed to be on duty *full time* in this ward, not just when it takes your fancy. There are patients waiting. Get cracking!'

A houseman beckoned her. 'Will you take my patient to a dresser, please, he'll need to have a plaster on his leg.'

Hilary fetched a wheelchair and when she had taken the patient to the plaster room she went to deal with admissions, treating black eyes, removing splinters and bathing cuts. It was one of those days when there were numerous casualties, but fortunately nothing very serious, but they were time-consuming.

She took some X-ray pictures from the radiographer and handed them to a houseman whose patient was suffering abdominal pain. Then she went to report to Sister Denvers that she was off duty.

Sister Denvers sat in her office whose walls were covered with stick-on notices, chiefly of the 'do not' variety, and Hilary thought flippantly that they had doubtless been ordered by Dr Sanders—undoubtedly he would be at the bottom of them.

'Well, Wilson?' Sister didn't look a pretty sight with her bulging green eyes and wisps of greying hair escaping from her bun.

'Reporting that I'm now off duty, Sister Denvers,' Hilary said demurely.

She watched hypnotised, as the already bulbous eyes seemed to protrude even further. Would they ever fall out?

'Off duty? That's out of the question. I'm already short-staffed.' Sister Denvers picked up her pen and began to write as if that was the end of the matter.

Hilary was appalled. She couldn't possibly let Nick down again, and at such short notice.

'I'm sorry, Sister, but I have an important appointment which I can't break,' she said firmly.

'Indeed? I'm afraid you'll have to.' Sister

Denvers appeared to swell and seemed about to burst.

From the corner of her eye Hilary saw Carol covering a grin by placing her hand on an apparently painful cheek. If it came to a showdown, Hilary decided, she would leave the hospital and work for Nick. Maybe this was the spur she needed to make the move.

'That's impossible, Sister Denvers. I *must* go.'

Sister Denvers stood up, a large, lumbering figure who dwarfed Hilary.

'Do I take it that you disobey my order?'

Hilary felt the colour recede from her face. 'I'm sorry, but I must,' she said stubbornly.

She heard somebody walking towards them and instinctively glanced over her shoulder. Her heart gave a convulsive lurch when she saw that it was Steve. No doubt he would be on her side after that friendly afternoon they had spent together, but she was embarrassed that he should be there when she was being told off by Sister.

But when she saw his eyes she was dismayed, for they were coldly disapproving—indeed, there was almost a look of dislike in them, something she had never seen in them before, not even with obstructive patients.

'You'll hear more of this, Nurse Wilson,' Sister Denvers threatened, although her voice held a more gentle tone now that Steve Sanders was here.

Hilary walked determinedly away. She would show them! She'd work for Nick and they could jolly well keep their job. She had to wait for stretchers to pass and heard Sister Denvers say,

'These girls who come over here for an extended holiday and condescend to put in a few hours' work when it suits them get up my nose!'

Then Dr Sanders' rich, carrying voice. 'Come now, there *are* good nurses who come over from England. It's the ones from wealthy backgrounds who are the trouble.'

Hilary's eyes blurred. It was so unfair. She had frequently stayed on duty after she should have left if the occasion warranted it. And even now, despite Nick, she would have stayed if there was a major disaster, but they could cope without her today unless something unexpected turned up, and even then they could summon assistance from other wards.

Steve's remark about girls from wealthy backgrounds hurt her, since she believed it was aimed directly at her. Yet she only had herself to blame for pretending to him about her home. She wondered why some people—like Carol—could tell lies ad infinitum and get away with it, whereas whenever she told even a half-truth it always seemed to land her in trouble.

She didn't feel so happy and excited about the afternoon's outing now; they had ruined it for her. She didn't want Steve to think badly of her, she had felt immense pleasure when he thanked her for the afternoon they had spent together, and although she knew he would have invited any nurse who happened to have been working with him, nevertheless it had been *her,* and they had been friendly and talked together and she had thought he too had enjoyed it. Now it seemed all that had gone, and he disapproved of her and believed she had come to Spain merely to have a good time with Nick.

Nick! Oh goodness, time was passing. She hurriedly changed into a sun-dress and in case they should go swimming put a bikini in her holdall, changed into sandals and set off for his office.

Nick's office was as bright and flamboyant as he was himself. The carpet was orange and the paintwork light green. The unnecessary curtains were patterned with sunflowers and protected from the sun with shutters. Nick leaned nonchalantly back in his chair, his legs crossed. His yellow hair, way-out clothes and lively personality made him the focal point, he was the sunflower and his assistants the leaves and stalk.

He was speaking on the telephone, raised his hand in smiling greeting to Hilary, then continued twisting his gold neck chains around his fingers as he continued his conversation. Fred and John, his negotiators, greeted Hilary pleasantly, and Sarah, his secretary, was friendly and hoped Hilary would have a pleasant afternoon.

Hilary was fascinated as she watched Nick and listened to his voice, which was sometimes enthusiastic, always friendly and again deadly serious, which must have influenced the caller. When he replaced the receiver his smiling concern vanished as if it had been drawn on his face with chalk, then wiped off with a duster.

He greeted Hilary as if she was the nicest thing that had ever entered his life.

'Aren't I the lucky one? All this and Hilary too,' he smiled, his brown eyes laughing and friendly.

'You certainly are,' said Fred. 'Don't forget it's my turn tomorrow.'

Hilary looked at him in surprise. 'Don't worry,' he laughed. 'My young lady is coming on a visit and I'll expect to have time off.'

Nick tossed a dossier on to his desk. 'And so you shall. In the meantime earn your bread today. Do the necessary with that.'

'Which one is this?' asked Fred, lifting the receiver as the telephone rang, and looking at Nick enquiringly.

'The Chalmers.'

'Aldebury Court?'

Nick nodded. 'They're paying the asking price too.'

Fred whistled silently, then replaced the receiver. 'Wrong number. That asking price—bit steep, wasn't it?'

Nick flicked open a file to check the price. 'Mm. Yes. Good, isn't it?'

'Depends which client you're thinking about.'

Nick shrugged. 'I've got to do the best I can for all my clients.'

'The Chalmers will be a bit pushed at that price.'

'True, but that's their problem. Anyhow, it's all settled now.' Nick locked his drawer. 'I'm off now with Hilary, but I'll look in later on to see if there are any calls.'

'Righto, have a good time. Cheerio.'

They all looked up to smile at Hilary as she walked towards the door. When they reached it Nick turned back.

'Oh, Sarah, a couple of old biddies—a Miss Quick and Miss Bell—may come in to ask about curtains and whatnot. Take them to Crofts and make sure that whoever's in charge there knows that I sent them. Okay?'

They drove off through the town in his elegant Mercedes. Hilary felt privileged and as excited and carefree as if she was starting on a holiday.

'Where are we going?' she asked.

He gave her a caressing smile. 'Just you wait and see. It'll bring a sparkle to your eyes, I promise you that. And they can do with it—you're looking whacked. Come on, Hilary, admit it, you're fed up with nursing, aren't you? Ready to come in with me?'

Despite her earlier decision to leave the hospital she found herself dithering again.

'No, you don't understand. I really like nursing. I don't say that I like all the people who work there, but it's so rewarding when you have patients coming in ill and unhappy and then you see them going home cured.'

'I bet that's not so rewarding as when I make a good sale. Do you get paid more if someone recovers?'

'Oh really, Nick,' Hilary protested, 'of course not!'

'So where's the reward?'

'How can I possibly explain? But can't you understand? Take that little girl I told you about, the one involved in the road accident last Saturday and who Dr Sanders was worried sick about. Well, she'd lost so much blood and gone through so much surgery we didn't hold out much hope for her. And today I heard that she was holding her own. That's worth a million dollars.'

Nick frowned impatiently. 'For heaven's sake, honey, this is our afternoon off, don't talk about such morbid things! No wonder you look peaky, with your mind always on sick people. Forget it, and remember we've been put on this earth to get as much enjoyment as we can, that's what the good Lord intended. If we don't do that nobody's going to give us a medal for being miserable.'

Of course Nick was right. She really must take his cheerful advice. As they drove along his remarks about the other drivers and his seemingly never-ending supply of jokes kept her giggling like a schoolgirl. Everything was enjoyable, the sun, the scenery, the laughter and the feeling of impending excitement.

He drew into a large car park, encircling it to find a vacant space.

'Right,' he said, when he had done so. 'Out you get.'

'What is it? An open-air theatre?' asked Hilary.

Nick put an arm around her shoulders and laughed down at her.

'Better than that, it's something you'll really enjoy. Your first ever bullfight.'

Hilary went rigid. 'A bullfight? You're having me on!' She looked up at him aghast. 'You're not? But it's revolting, I couldn't possibly watch it!'

His eyebrows shot up. 'Rubbish! You've never seen one, have you?'

'No, and I'm not going to now. I—I couldn't. It's cruel, it's vicious, and I didn't think anyone decent went to them.'

'Come on, honey, they're exciting and great fun, I promise you. The bull enjoys it as much as the matador.'

'How can you possibly believe that?'

'It's a sport, like boxing. You don't go all peculiar at the thought of a boxing match, do you? Come on, let your hair down. Relax!'

Hilary faced him, her blue eyes wide and tragic. 'I'm sorry, Nick, I feel mean spoiling your afternoon when you thought it would be a treat for me. You watch it by all means, if that's your idea of enjoyment. I'll go for a walk and meet you afterwards. Have you any idea what time that will be?'

His eyes narrowed and his mouth looked cruel. 'You've got double standards, honey. Why all this fuss about a spot of blood and gore when all the time you're dying to talk about it? Take that kid in the road accident. Given the chance you'd have told me every bloody detail——'

'Shut up!' Hilary covered her ears with her hands. 'Shut up!' She was seeing the mutilated body of the little girl, the agony in Steve's eyes, and remembering the vicarious pain he suffered even when he was off duty.

Nick's mood suddenly changed. He took her face in his hands.

'Kiss me, anyhow,' he said fondly. 'And if you don't want to see a bullfight then you shan't.'

She looked at him in surprise. 'And you really don't mind?'

'No. I meant it as a treat for you, but feeling as you do it's a non-starter, isn't it? So let's not spoil the day by arguing. What else can we do?' He thought for a moment. 'I know, we'll drive to the jetty and you can do a spot of paragliding. How does that grab you?'

Truth to tell, it filled Hilary with absolute horror, but she dared not turn down this suggestion too. She forced a smile and said with as much enthusiasm as she could muster up, 'Oh—great.'

She was quiet on the journey, and although she automatically responded to Nick's remarks her thoughts were on herself. She was a dull sort of girl and not a bit like the sun-bronzed, laughing girls in revealing bikinis in the travel brochures who swam and sailed and rode donkeys. Tessa would soon have become just like them, she had the flair, the sense of adventure. Hilary wished she could be more like her.

As it was, when she joined the queue of people waiting on the jetty she felt horribly aware of her pale skin, her modest bikini and the icy block where her stomach should be. It was but small comfort that she was wearing a life-jacket, because the parachute felt like a bird of prey on her back, full of evil intentions.

When it was her turn a rope from the motor-boat was attached to her waist. People standing behind her held her parachute aloft as the engine of the boat started up.

'Off you go,' they said, and gave her a slight push.

She ran a few steps forward, then as the rope tightened she shot up into the air, leaving her stomach behind her. Then something incredible happened. She soared up and down through the air like a human kite, seeing the panoramic view below and experiencing the most wonderful feeling of weightlessness and peace and quiet. If only she could stay up here for ever! But all too soon the engine of the motor-boat stopped and she fell through the air, hitting the water with an almighty splash before coming to the surface and floating on the sea. Then she was hauled on to the boat and taken back to the jetty.

Nick was standing there, bronzed and handsome, his teeth gleaming white as he laughed down at her.

'That wasn't as bad as you feared it was going to be, was it?'

'Oh no, it was the loveliest feeling. It was fantastic,' smiled Hilary, hugging herself.

'And you thought it was going to be dreadful?'

'How did you know?'

'By the look on your face beforehand. I've got some super pictures I took of you looking scared to death.'

'You didn't!'

'Mm. And I should be able to sell them somewhere,' he said.

'Don't be daft!'

'A satirical magazine might take them,' he said thoughtfully.

'You wouldn't!' protested Hilary.

His eyes sparkled devilishly. 'That depends on how much they were willing to pay.'

Hilary bit her lip. She felt pretty certain he was quite capable of doing that. Making money, regardless of how he did so, was a fair way of life to him.

'So you enjoyed it?' he smiled.

'Yes, it was marvellous.'

'Honey, there are all kinds of things you haven't tried, and believe me, they're all enjoyable. Team up with me and I'll teach you how to enjoy life. And that includes lovemaking. I bet that's new to you too.'

At his words Hilary felt an erotic thrill, temptation, excitement, but above all embarrassment and a feeling of inadequacy as if she didn't know the best way of replying to him. She thought it was safest to laugh.

'You never give up, do you?' she smiled.

When she had dressed and they were driving back, Nick said,

'One night I was driving along this road when I saw a car slow down and a chap in the front seat leaned out and snatched a woman's handbag as she was walking past.'

Hilary swung around to look at him. 'How awful for her! Poor woman!'

'I shouted out to her to stay where she was, then I reversed and drove after them for a couple of miles until I was able to ram their car. The chaps—there were two of them—jumped out and started to run away. I went after them, but when they saw I was alone they turned on me and one of them whipped out a knife.'

'Oh, Nick! They could have killed you. What did you do? Get back in your car?'

'No chance! I gave them a couple of karate kicks and left them lying on the ground no doubt wondering where the hell they were.'

'How exciting! Just like a film. So did you get

the handbag?' Hilary looked at him with wide-eyed admiration.

'Yes. I picked it up and drove back to where the lady was still standing, would you believe! You should have seen her face when I handed the bag over.' He threw back his head and laughed. 'She even offered me some pesetas as a reward.'

'Oh, Nick, you didn't take them, did you?'

'No. I said, "Thank you, dear lady, but I'll settle for a kiss." However, when she came closer I realised I'd made one hell of a mistake and no way was I going to kiss that dame. She was at least twenty years older than I'd thought. So I put my foot down and, honey, you couldn't see me for dust!'

Hilary couldn't stop laughing. 'I bet you're still regretting refusing those pesetas,' she said.

'Too right I am!'

When she had thought it over again she said, 'So you can do karate? That's useful.'

'Oh yes,' he said nonchalantly. 'Actually I'm a black belt.'

They stopped off at Nick's office where he made a couple of phone calls in his private room.

'Have you been somewhere nice?' Sarah asked Hilary.

'Oh yes, I went para-gliding for the first time, it was great. Have you done it?'

Sarah shook her head. 'No, I'm not keen on

the idea. I like to keep my feet on terra firma, thanks very much!'

'That's how I felt until Nick persuaded me to do it,' Hilary told her. 'He's so wonderfully athletic himself, isn't he?'

'Is he?'

'Oh yes. Didn't you know? He's an Olympic swimmer and a karate black belt. And goodness knows what else!'

'Do you hear that?' Sarah turned to Fred and John, who were already laughing.

Hilary looked at them questioningly.

Fred said, 'Don't worry, I'm sure he'll tell you in his own good time.'

When they left the office Nick said they would drive to his new apartment, which Hilary hadn't yet seen. It was situated halfway up a cliff so that buildings between there and the sea would not obstruct the view. It was beautifully fitted out with large air-conditioned rooms and marble floors. From the large windows, fringed by trees, she saw a key-shaped swimming pool and way down below was the sandy beach and the sea, which rolled gently inland and then splashed on the rocks.

'Let me see the kitchen,' she said, but Nick caught her round the waist.

'First things first—you haven't seen my bedroom.'

She gasped at the size of it. 'You're got room for half a dozen beds in it!' she exclaimed.

He forced her back on to the bed, and pinning

her by her shoulders said, as he looked into her eyes, 'I only want one.' Then his mouth covered hers and she felt helpless.

When he paused for breath she took the opportunity of turning her head aside.

'And do you know what I want?' she asked breathlessly.

'Tell me,' he murmured, his hand roaming over her body.

'I want something to eat,' she said plaintively. 'I'm starving!'

He let her go. 'You certainly know how to kill romance, honey!' he said ruefully.

'I don't know about that, but I really do feel hungry.'

He looked at her through narrowed eyes. 'I think I know the game you're playing. But it's a game two can play.'

The nice thing about Nick was that he never seemed to hold a grudge for long, and soon he was his usual friendly, laughing self.

They drove to their usual restaurant and were looking for a table when once again Nick spotted Steve Sanders and Wendy Smith. With a friendly wave as if he had know them for years he steered Hilary in their direction. Remembering Steve's disapproval earlier on and now the fact that he would have guessed aright about her urgent appointment, she avoided looking at him.

'This is a stroke of luck, two empty seats at your table—may we join you?' asked Nick.

Hilary would have given anything at all to

have been alone in the canteen rather than have this happen. But Steve gave a small smile and said he would be delighted

Nick handed Hilary a menu, and said to the others,

'Never attempt to make love on an empty stomach. I was about to have a romantic interlude with Hilary and at the last moment what did she say? "I'm starving!" Now, Steve, wouldn't you call that a real passion-killer?'

Hilary was furious. Her face turned scarlet, but there was no way she could correct his version of the event. Suddenly her appetite left her completely.

Steve looked at her intently and there was understanding in his eyes.

'Maybe you picked the wrong girl,' he said casually to Nick. Then he spoke to Hilary. 'Did you eat any lunch?'

She couldn't speak, she just shook her head.

'That's not too clever after a busy morning. You must eat something now.'

She just wanted to die, she had never felt more miserable in her life.

'I'll have a salad,' she said unhappily.

'No,' said Steve, taking the menu off her. 'You'd do better with an omelette. A ham omelette.'

She was about to refuse, he had no right to tell her what she must eat, but the waiter appeared and the order was given.

Steve, of course, was right, and when she had

eaten she felt much better, and able to join in the general conversation.

Wendy told them that she was studying medicine and had come to Spain for a holiday.

'And where are you staying?' asked Nick.

'With Steve,' she replied casually.

Instinctively Hilary looked at Steve, knowing that he had a flat at the hospital where visiting females would not be tolerated.

'My mother has an apartment she's lent us,' he explained.

'Whereabouts is it?' asked Nick.

'Just outside Marbella,' Steve replied.

Nick looked impressed. 'That's a nice area, the properties fetch good prices.'

As they discussed the merits of Spain Hilary remained silent, taking in the knowledge that Steve's mother obviously approved of Wendy and was doing her best to encourage the romance. Wendy was a pleasant down-to-earth girl who would no doubt make a good doctor, but Hilary was surprised that she was Steve's choice, for she believed he should have somebody more gentle and loving, after what he had told her of his childhood. But of course she hardly knew her, and in any case, how could you decide which person was right for someone else? It was difficult enough to sort out your own problems. Take her and Nick, for example. He said he loved her, but would she be the right wife for him? And would he be right for her?

'Before Wendy returns home we're hoping to

take a coach tour of mountain villages, stopping each night at a *parador*. Have you any experience of that?' Steve asked Nick.

'I've never been on a tour, I prefer to drive myself, but I've seen quite a lot of the villages. It's a nice area.'

'I like to drive as a rule, but as my time here is running out I thought I'd be able to enjoy the scenery more if I left the driving to somebody else. That way I can talk to my companion, too. Well, come along, love, I think it's time we were leaving.'

'I hope you enjoy the trip,' Hilary said to Wendy, as she rose to her feet.

'I've been told I will,' she smiled. 'It's Steve's idea.'

'I mustn't let her go back ignorant of what Spain is really like. You can lie out in the sun anywhere.'

'That's true,' Wendy said amiably.

So he was laying down the law again. He'd probably make the poor girl write a thesis on each place they visited. Fancy having to put up with a bossy man like that all your life, Hilary thought—then wondered why she felt so sad.

CHAPTER SEVEN

HILARY never knew whether or not Sister Denvers was responsible, but she was moved to another ward. In a way she was sorry, for she liked the quick turnover of patients and the sense of urgency in Casualty, but Sister Denvers had been becoming increasingly difficult to please.

'Off to Ward Five, Wilson, and I wish them joy of you,' she said with a sniff.

'You mean I'm moving there?' Hilary asked in surprise.

'Well, Ward Five isn't moving down here to save you the trouble,' Sister snapped, stalking back to her room.

Hilary, feeling suitably snubbed, looked around at the cubicles and the rows of chairs with a feeling of sadness.

'Wakey, wakey!' Carol came up behind her and pounced. 'How are things?'

'Denvers has managed to get rid of me,' Hilary said mournfully.

'You haven't been kicked out?' asked Carol in alarm.

'Out of Casualty, I have. I'm being sent to Ward Five.'

'Weren't you told when you came here you'd probably be moved somewhere else?'

'Oh yes,' Hilary said with some relief, 'so I was, I'd forgotten that. Which is Ward Five?'

'It used to be Women's Medical, now it's the lot. Medical, surgical and for men and women.'

'That doesn't sound too bad. Could be nice and busy. I only hope the Sister won't turn out to be Denvers' twin.'

'They couldn't make two like her,' Carol assured her.

'Nurse Jenks!' Sister Denvers bellowed.

'There she blows!' grinned Carol, and went to do her bidding.

Ward Five was large, with the beds pushed close together to accommodate as many patients as possible, which did nothing to ensure their privacy, although economically it made sense.

Hilary nodded to one or two of the nurses as she made her way to the Sister's room. She had chatted to one or two of them on occasion in the staff room or canteen but had not struck up a friendship with any of them.

Sister Denvers' poor opinion of her would undoubtedly have preceded her, so it was with a feeling of apprehension that she knocked on the door.

'Come in.'

Hilary stared for a moment at the trim, middle-aged Sister with a pleasant, motherly expression.

'Sister Prowse! It isn't—it can't be!' she

exclaimed, her face wreathed in a smile.

'Hilary, you're the last person I expected to see. How do you come to be over here?' Pat Prowse kissed her fondly.

'I couldn't get anything I wanted in England, but I've only recently come here. I've been in Casualty, and aren't I glad to move here with you!' Hilary smiled.

'And aren't I glad to have you!'

'When did *you* come to Spain, Pat?'

'It's nearly three years now. Not long after you did your midwifery with me.'

'I enjoyed that. It seems a long time ago.'

'And you're a staff nurse now—that's good.'

'It's why I had to move from the Memorial,' Hilary explained. 'They hadn't any more vacancies for staff nurses.'

'That's the way it goes, I always think that's a pity. So you're not married yet?' Sister Prowse glanced at her hand.

'No, I'm afraid not.' Hilary smiled.

'What about a boy-friend?'

'No again. It's all the studying, I didn't have time for a social life. I'm not all that bright and it was a hard slog.'

Sister Prowse laid her hand on her shoulder. 'You'll meet the right man one day.'

She herself had been widowed after a brief marriage and was now dedicated to nursing. Her great regret was that she had no children. If she could have had a wish granted it would have been to have a daughter like Hilary, unsophisticated and kind.

There was a short rap on the door followed by Steve Sanders' voice.

'May I come in? Hello, Pat. And hello, Nurse Wilson. Are you working here now?'

'Yes.' Hilary looked up into his fascinating blue eyes and smiled.

'And aren't I glad to have her,' Pat said fondly.

'You're old friends?'

'Yes. Hilary came to St Vincent's when I was there to do her midwifery training. I knew then that she was going to be an excellent nurse or a mother, she was so good with those babies.'

Steve raised his eyebrows. 'Well now, there's a tribute!'

'And here she is, fancy free at—what is it? Twenty-two—I don't know what's the matter with young men, they don't know what they're missing.'

'No young man? Is that what she's led you to believe?' smiled Steve.

'Hilary's told me she hasn't got a boy-friend, and I believe her,' Pat said loyally. Then she picked up the telephone. 'Coffee, please, Nurse.' Glancing at Hilary, she added, 'For three, please.'

Hilary felt pleased and embarrassed at being included in their talk. Normally coffee in Sister's room was for herself and the visiting doctor, never before had she known a staff nurse to be in there with them.

She found she learned a lot about the patients by listening to them discussing their problems, and when she later accompanied them on the round she was able to know about the patients and to appreciate Steve's charming bedside manner. Time seemed to be of no importance as he gave each patient his undivided attention.

Mrs Thorne looked wan and depressed after having recently had a gall bladder operation.

'It's natural to feel a bit low after that operation, Mrs Thorne. You'll feel quite different in a few days' time, I promise you.' He smiled at her reassuringly.

She plucked at the sheet. 'It's the indecision that's getting me down, Doctor.' She raised worried eyes to his.

'Tell me,' he said softly, sitting on the edge of her bed.

'Well, it's like this. My husband and I came out here to buy a flat, we'd put our house in Chertsey up for sale, and I was very keen on the idea, I must confess. Until now.'

Steve nodded and waited for her to continue.

'I've been feeling so ill and miserable, and I'd just like to be back home where I know everybody and everywhere. I don't think I can face up to the effort of moving.' She dabbed her eyes with a tissue.

Steve took her hand and held it. 'Of course, that's only natural. An operation is a shock to the mind and the body, and both need time to recuperate. You mustn't attempt to come to a decision until you're up and about again.'

She looked up at him gratefully. 'Thank you, Doctor, you've set my mind at rest. I thought I was just being silly.'

'On the contrary, you'd be foolish to come to any decision at the moment.'

He gave her a devastating smile, reached in his pocket and held out a stone on the palm of his hand.

'This is what you wanted, this rather pretty little stone which caused all the trouble. What are you going to do with it?'

She leaned forward to examine it. 'I'm sure I don't know, but I'll show it to my husband. I bet he'll be surprised to see how big it is.'

'Then I'll leave it with you.' Steve placed it on a wad of cottonwool and put it on her locker.

He moved on to the next patient, who had had an appendicectomy. The girl had a tube leading from her wound to a bottle on the floor. She was attractive and pouted provocatively at Steve.

'You told me that having my appendix out was a simple operation which would only take a few minutes. Were you deliberately telling a lie, or did you make a mistake?'

He checked the readings on her chart before letting his eyes wander over her as he assessed her general condition.

'A straightforward appendicectomy is as I described it, and that's what you had. But then you sprang an abscess on us, didn't you? You're a naughty girl, you shouldn't do things like that. How are you feeling?'

She wrinkled her nose. 'Rotten. Fed up. How long is this wretched tube going to be kept in? It makes me feel subhuman!'

Steve looked at Pat. 'How long has it been in, Sister?'

'Coming up to forty hours, Doctor.'

'Then it can be removed this evening, Anne, if it's still running clear.'

'And can I get out of this place then?'

'No, not just yet. Aren't we making you comfortable?'

'Hospitals are never comfortable. I want to lie in the sun, it's such a waste of time being stuck in here.' Anne fluttered her eyelashes at him.

'Illness is always a waste of time, but it's something we sometimes have to put up with,' Steve said quietly. 'We'll discharge you when we think the time is right. In the meantime be a good girl.' He patted her shoulder and walked away.

Hilary, glancing back at her, saw her poke her tongue out at Steve's receding figure. She felt a certain amount of sympathy for her and smiled and gave a little wave.

Steve, who missed nothing, said wryly, 'You have a fellow-feeling for her, Nurse?'

Hilary looked at him questioningly. 'I have?'

'You both want to lie in the sun and neither of you likes to be told what's good for you.' His eyes challenged her and she turned aside. Would he never forget that incident?

'Ah, Mrs Blewett,' he said to another patient. 'Your sugar balance is right now, so we can get on with your cataract removal. I think we'll put you down for the day after tomorrow,' he smiled.

'That's good, Doctor. And you say it isn't a very serious operation?' she asked anxiously.

'Not nowadays, but you must play your part. Eat whatever is given you—every bit of it—and don't take any sugar at all. Never forget or let anyone else forget that you're a diabetic.'

The day went remarkably quickly and pleasantly under Sister Prowse, and Hilary felt happy and relaxed when she met Nick in the evening. After their meal in their favourite restaurant they strolled down to the promenade, their arms entwined.

'Next time you have a day off we'll go up in a hot air balloon, you'll enjoy that,' he said.

'That'll be marvellous. You know, I've never done any sport in my life, I never had the opportunity. Now I'm beginning to realise what I've missed,' Hilary admitted.

He held her closer. 'You're still missing out on the best things in life because you're scared. You're stuck in that hospital when you should be with me. We could have a super time. Don't worry about the future, that doesn't do any good at all.'

'But I think I'm really going to enjoy working with Sister Prowse.' Then, to change the subject, Hilary went on, 'There was a patient in my ward whom you might know, a Mrs Thorne.'

'Thorne? Why should I know her? Did she mention me?'

'No, but she said she and her husband had come over here to buy a flat, but since she's been in hospital she's had second thoughts and just wants to get back home. I can understand that, can't you?'

'Mr and Mrs Thorne? Yes, they're on the point of signing the contract. What's her trouble?' Nick asked seriously.

'She's had a gall bladder op—been feeling pretty low after it, but she'll soon buck up, I expect.'

He nodded. 'Good. So you're happier in your ward? That's great. Oh, if I should want to get in touch with you, what's your ward number?'

'Five. Under Sister Prowse.'

They walked down to the promenade and looked out to sea.

'Doesn't it look lovely?' sighed Hilary. 'Do you know what I'd like? I'd like to be on a cruise with nothing around but water, water everywhere and the smell of the sea air.'

'You've got yourself a deal, honey. We can't go on a cruise tonight, but we'll take a boat out and you can pretend,' said Nick.

It seemed they were the only people on the vast expanse of calm sea. Hilary let her hands trail in the water as she leaned back, enjoying the slight breeze on her face. Then the moon rose, bathing everywhere with golden light. It was a fairytale trip.

When they got back they went into a different wine bar for a drink.

'To pretend we're somewhere else, somewhere exotic,' Nick laughed.

'When I'm in England Spain seems exotic. Now that I'm here it's got to be somewhere else. Is it always like that, Nick?'

'I guess so, or what's a heaven for?' he said lightly.

When he was leaving her at the hospital Hilary said, 'It's been one of the nicest evenings I've ever had, Nick.'

'And you could come back with me and make it *the* nicest,' he murmured, his lips on hers.

After submitting to his kisses for a moment or two she laughed and struggled free.

He put his hands on her shoulders. 'Still no dice?'

'Not yet, Nick,' she said apologetically.

'Then I suppose I'll have to keep on trying,' he said, and cheerfully walked away.

As she undressed in her room Hilary felt a little worried. Would his persistence win in the end? Would the time come when she felt so happy in his company that she would let go of her principles, leave the work she enjoyed, disappoint her parents and go to him? She sighed. Why couldn't she be like Tessa, let the future take care of itself and enjoy the happiness he could give her?

In the morning when Hilary came on duty Sister Prowse told her there had been an admission during the night, a Mr Long, a fifty-year-old man with severe chest pain, in the bed next to Mrs Thorne.

'Leave him for the time being, Dr Sanders will be coming up to see him in a few minutes,' Sister Prowse said.

Hilary was wrapping the cuff of the sphygmomanometer around Anne's arm.

'So you've got your tube out, that's a step in the right direction,' she said.

'I suppose so, but I still feel rotten.'

'Your blood pressure is okay, so you'll soon start feeling bet——' Hilary stopped in mid-sentence as she saw Nick enter the ward carrying a beautiful bouquet. Her heart thumped. He shouldn't have brought it here. Was this the beginning of an all-out campaign? It was embarrassing, because any minute now Steve Sanders would arrive.

She hurried towards him, frowning. 'Nick, you shouldn't have come here,' she whispered.

'Hello, honey! Hard at it? It's nice to see where you work.'

'You shouldn't have,' she said again,

'Why not? I've come to visit a friend. Tell me, where's Mrs Thorne? Oh, there you are!'

He greeted her with a clever combination of a smile and a look of anxiety. 'How are you feeling today, Mrs Thorne? I've been worried about you.'

He laid the beautiful flowers on her bed. She looked from them to him.

'Are they really for me? They're beautiful! I've never had a bouquet like this before. You *are* kind. How did you know I was here?'

'Nurse Wilson told me. She said you were feeling a bit low, so I thought I'd try and cheer you up.'

She picked up the flowers to admire them again. 'You've certainly done that, Mr Trowbridge. But on the other hand you've made me feel very guilty at letting everybody down. But the truth is, I want to go home.' Her mouth trembled.

Nick pulled up a chair and took both her hands in his. 'Of course you feel like that, you're weak and depressed. I know I would be after an operation like that. I was speaking to your husband only today, and he's been very worried about you. What's bucked him up no end is knowing you're going to live here. When you're settled in with everything nice and new—and don't forget the sunshine, that's thrown in for free as a bonus—you'll feel a different person, and I'm sure you'll both be very happy.'

'My husband is still keen on living here, I suppose,' she said slowly.

'Yes, he certainly is, for your sake as much

as his. You're a very lucky lady to have such a caring husband. Do you know, I believe he'd even give up the idea of living here if that was what you wanted, but I know you love him too much to let him do that, don't you?'

Mrs Thorne chewed her bottom lip. 'That's a point. I hadn't thought of it like that. I suppose I'm getting selfish in my old age,' she said with a rueful smile.

He shook his head. 'Never! When I first saw you both do you know what I thought?'

She shook her head.

'I thought what a lucky couple you were to be so considerate of each other. You don't see it all that often. Either the wife or the husband wants their own way. But not you two'

She smiled. 'Well, I suppose we do get on pretty well. Yes, I'm lucky, Claude's always been good to me.'

'And you to him. And you to him.' Nick opened his briefcase and took out some brochures and forms. 'I'll leave these with you so you can browse through them and see again how attractive these apartments are. And this one—' he laid it on top of the others, 'is the one you sign. Down there, where I've pencilled in a cross. And in case you didn't bring in a pen, and I don't suppose you did, have this with my compliments.' He handed her an orange-coloured ballpoint pen with his name written down the side in green.

'I'll pop in again very soon, and in the meantime I'll tell your good husband that I've seen you. Any message for him? Just your love? Well, he couldn't ask for anything better.' He took her hand in both of his as he bade her goodbye. Then he looked across the ward and waved and smiled at Hilary before leaving.

Her arms felt as heavy as lead, no way could she have waved back. Indeed, she was filled with embarrassment for all this while Steve had been at the bedside of Mr Lock and must have heard every word of their conversation. Why should that embarrass her? She wasn't sure exactly, but it was something to do with Nick's effusiveness. She was glad he had not seen Steve, whose back had been turned to him. He straightened up now and on seeing Hilary beckoned to her with an imperious forefinger.

She came across immediately. 'Yes, Doctor?'

'Outside, if you please, Nurse,' he said sternly.

She followed him to Sister's office and he held the door open for her. Pat wasn't there, and Hilary didn't know whether to be sorry or glad. A private conversation with Steve was something she would enjoy. She smiled up at him, but the smile froze on her face. His face was dark with anger, his unsmiling eyes almost unrecognisable.

'Nurse Wilson, how dare you discuss one of our patients with an outsider!' he grated furiously.

'I—I didn't,' she faltered. 'I only happened to mention——'

'Countries have fallen because some foolish person has just "happened to mention" a piece of private information. I'm extremely disappointed and angry to think that one of our nurses who should know better has broken our rule of confidentiality in an attempt to further her boy-friend's financial interests. Let there be no more of this!'

Hilary felt that everything inside her was sliding downward. She tried to raise her eyes to look at him, but her lashes flickered, then fell again. She knew that her lips were trembling and she wanted to cry.

'Have I made myself quite clear?' His voice was pitiless.

She gave a small careful nod so that her tears wouldn't fall. At that he left her abruptly as if afraid of what he might say next. She steadied herself against Pat's desk, wiped her eyes, then went back to the ward.

Steve Sanders was already at Mrs Thorne's bedside. His voice was entirely different now, it was gentle and caring, not gushing as Nick's had been, but with a serious, authoritative undertone.

'Now, Mrs Thorne, I believe your estate agent has brought you some forms to sign regarding the property you were thinking of buying before you fell ill?'

'That's right, Doctor, and look at those beautiful flowers he's brought me! He's so kind, you can't imagine. And he made me realise that

I was being—well, selfish, I suppose, in changing my mind.'

Steve waited for her to say more. 'He reminded me how much my husband wanted to stay here, and I think he does. So——' She picked up the brochures and forms and looked at them unhappily.

Steve took them from her gently but firmly, folded them and put them away in her locker.

'Mrs Thorne,' he said quietly, 'you're not to look at those brochures or sign anything while you're in this hospital. Do you understand?'

She looked perplexed. 'I don't know. Mr Trowbridge tells me to sign them, I think my husband would like me to, and you come along and tell me not to. How am I to know what to do for the best?'

'What you do when you leave this hospital is up to you, I have no say in the matter. But I'm in charge here and I forbid you to sign. In my opinion you're not in a fit condition to commit yourself in such an important matter.' Steve smiled gently. 'And don't worry about it, because the more you worry the longer your stay in here will be. I'm being serious, Mrs Thorne—there's to be no signing of contracts, that's doctor's orders!'

He left her then, and although Hilary knew he must have seen her he walked past her as if she did not exist. She had been going to put the lovely flowers in water, but suddenly they seemed utterly distasteful and she left them for another nurse to attend to.

CHAPTER EIGHT

'THERE'LL be no Dr Sanders this morning,' Sister Prowse remarked as she poured some coffee for Hilary.

'Is he—all right?' Hilary looked at her anxiously.

Pat chuckled and squeezed her hand. 'Yes, he's quite all right. He's taken a week's leave and he and his friend are going on a coach tour before he leaves us.'

'Oh yes, he said they'd be doing a tour of the mountain villages. It sounds fascinating,' Hilary ended wistfully.

Pat seemed surprised. 'He told you?'

Hilary remembered with embarrassment the evening in the restaurant when Nick had insisted they join Steve and Wendy.

'Actually he told a friend of mine and I overheard,' she said.

'You've made a friend over here, then?'

'Yes.' Then because she knew that Pat was interested in everything she did, Hilary told her who he was.

'He's a local estate agent, Nick Trowbridge.'

'You mean that man who brought in those flowers for Mrs Thorne?'

'Yes, that's him,' Hilary agreed unwillingly.

'Oh dear! Steve was very annoyed about that. She'd better not sign those papers or he'll go spare. It was a bit much for your friend to try to persuade her, wasn't it?'

Hilary tried to make excuses for him. 'It depends on how you look at it. You see, he's built up a terrific business through his charm and persuasion and he—well, I don't think he knows where to stop.'

'Then I hope he knows where to stop in his personal relationships,' said Pat, looking hard at Hilary. 'I know the type.'

Hilary blushed a pretty pink. 'Oh, I know how to deal with him.'

'Hm, I wouldn't be too sure. It strikes me he could be pretty ruthless. Watch out for him, my dear, I wouldn't like to see you hurt.'

'There's no fear of that,' Hilary assured her. Then, with a rush of affection, she said, 'It's lovely working with you again. It was hell with Sister Denvers in Casualty.'

'Bridie's bark is worse than her bite,' Pat said.

'Bridie? Is that her name? It doesn't suit her at all.'

'It's Bridget really. She's not got a lot to be amiable about. She lives with a sister who's a very difficult invalid, and poor old Bridie doesn't get a break at all. We've suggested that she puts her sister in a home, but she won't even consider that. She says they've always been very close and she can't send her away now.'

'Oh dear! Poor thing. I wish I'd known, I'd have felt differently about her.'

'Most people have their problems, and you don't find them wearing a placard saying what they are.'

'I suppose not,' Hilary said slowly. 'The answer is to make excuses for everybody—but that isn't easy, is it?'

'And what led you to believe that life was easy?'

Hilary gave a wistful smile. 'I guess I just hoped it would be.'

Pat toyed with her teaspoon. 'Now Steve Sanders is a thoroughly nice man, he seems to have all the virtues without in any way being a prude,' she said, looking at Hilary hard.

'He—he can be very harsh, though. And he's bossy, he thinks he knows best about everything,' Hilary said mutinously, still smarting from the telling-off he had given her over Mrs Thorne.

'Harsh? I'm sure he isn't, not unless it's necessary. And of course he must think he knows best, it wouldn't do for him to seem unsure with a patient on the operating table, now would it? When you say bossy you mean authoritative, and of course he is, that makes him the man he is.' Obviously Pat wasn't going to tolerate a word being said against him, so Hilary had to agree.

'Well, back to work,' said Pat, pushing her cup aside. 'And if Mr Thorne or your friend comes in just you make sure Mrs Thorne doesn't sign anything.'

'Okay, I'll do my best, but I can't see myself laying down the law to them.'

'You'd better,' Pat warned.

Hilary took the cups and saucers to the kitchen to wash them. She stared out at the sunny blue sky and garden with longing. She wondered just where Steve and Wendy were at this moment, and envied them. She'd heard about the villages with the narrow cobbled streets and the small white cottages with doors that opened on to the street, so like in a Cornish village, the difference being that here there would be shutters and iron bars at the windows—and, of course, the sunshine. Perhaps one day Nick would take her to see them, but she doubted whether they would be his scene.

She returned to the ward, which was not going to be brightened up by Steve's arrival. She looked at the rows of beds with patients sitting beside them unless they were on drips or had a leg in traction.

Anne was up and dressed in a very revealing scarlet two-piece. She looked well, for there was colour on her cheeks and lips and mascara on her lashes.

Hilary stopped beside her. 'My, my, you're looking very dishy! So you must be feeling better.'

'Not entirely. When is Dr Sanders coming round? He's late this morning.'

'He's on leave, but another doctor will be here later on.'

'Another doctor? I don't want to see him, I want Dr Sanders,' Anne pouted.

'He won't be back until next week. Did you want to speak to him especially?'

She gave a saucy grin. 'You bet I do!'

'And what's that supposed to mean?' asked Hilary.

'It means, Nurse Prunes and Prisms, that I would hope our conversation would lead to something meaningful! The trouble is, you don't get a chance for a private talk in a cluttered-up ward like this.'

Hilary stared at her blankly. 'What *are* you talking about?'

'Come on now, don't pretend he doesn't turn you on.'

'I don't know what you mean,' said Hilary, her face flushing.

'He's so sexy, my BP soars when he looks at me in that special way as if he knows everything about me, even what I'm thinking.'

'He probably does. That's his job,' Hilary said coolly.

'Wouldn't I like to get him in bed with me!' said Anne fervently. 'What do you think would happen?'

'He would examine your wound to make sure it was healing satisfactorily,' Hilary replied, disliking this conversation.

Anne gave a hoot of derisive laughter. 'I'm

making you feel embarrassed, aren't I? But I know you feel the same as I do about him, it shows in your face. Oh—what's happened to Harry?'

'Harry?' Hilary swung around, to see Harry Long slumped across his chair, his face ashen. She sped across the ward and felt his pulse, then raced out of the ward calling.

'Cardiac arrest!'

Sister Prowse dialled the emergency number and within moments the team came running in. Hilary pulled the curtains around Harry's bed while a doctor thumped on his chest with a clenched fist, before beginning cardiac massage.

Hilary left them working on him and went to attend to the other patients. When eventually porters arrived and he was wheeled away Mrs Thorne called her over.

'Has—has he passed away?' she whispered fearfully.

'Oh no. He's okay now, but he's gone up to ICU so he can be monitored non-stop as a safety precaution,' Hilary replied.

'They knew he had a heart condition, shouldn't they have sent him there straight away?'

'Apparently it wasn't considered necessary, and of course they would know his history and act accordingly.'

'I must say they didn't waste any time coming to deal with him. Anyone would think they were waiting outside the door!'

Hilary smiled. 'Well, it's something like that, they're always on the alert, because time is so important in these matters. Tell me, what did your husband have to say about your gallstone?'

Mrs Thorne laughed. 'Men! He said I'd passed three babies all right, so why all the fuss about a small stone!'

'You want to point out that the stone wasn't in your womb! After that unfeeling remark the least he can do is to have the stone mounted in gold and made into a brooch for you to wear. It would make an excellent talking point at a dinner party,' Hilary laughed.

'Not for me, thank you. It was bad enough inside me, I certainly don't want to have it outside as well.'

'But you're feeling better now?' Hilary held her wrist to check her pulse.

'Oh, much better, more my old self. When do you think I'll be discharged?'

Hilary entered her reading on the chart. 'That's up to Dr Sanders.'

'He'll be around this morning, won't he?'

'No, I'm afraid not. He's on leave for a week.'

'A week!' gasped Mrs Thorne. 'That means I'll be here for another ten days or so?'

'Probably.'

'Oh dear! Everyone is getting impatient with me.'

'Never mind. No signing those papers, mind,' added Hilary.

Mrs Thorne gave a rueful smile. 'If I wasn't

so afraid of making Dr Sanders angry I would have signed. I've been under enough pressure, believe me.'

'From your husband?'

'Yes. And from Mr Trowbridge.' She smiled. 'He's very persuasive, isn't he? And very attractive. He's got a way with him, the sort of man who could sell ice-cream to Eskimos, as they say. But Dr Sanders—well, he's different again. I just have to do what he tells me. He's the boss.'

Hilary gave a wry smile. 'Yes, he's certainly the boss.'

The week dragged interminably. Even when she was out with Nick Hilary felt a bleakness at the prospect of returning to the hospital, which seemed completely empty without the possibility of seeing Steve at any moment. She had marked the days off in her diary and there were two more to go. Tomorrow he would be on the last lap of the tour and the following day he would have returned but not yet be back at the hospital.

She had checked the tour and knew that they would be coming back via Costella, which was only about an hour's drive away. How she envied Wendy! Secretly she wondered whether they had slept together at the *paradors* and guessed that they would have done. She tried to picture them together and ached with a fierce longing to have been in her place. She imagined Steve's arms around her, his naked body pressed against hers, his mouth covering hers and his eyes dark with passion. Momentarily she basked in this bliss, this ecstasy, while tremors of delight flowed through her like a tidal wave.

Then she forced her thoughts to Wendy, but couldn't imagine her melting in his arms; she would more likely tell him to take a cold shower and go for a run round the block. But actually, of course, she couldn't really be so cold and unloving, that was just a façade. Beneath that frigid exterior must beat a passionate heart, or how could Steve have become attracted to her? Unless he preferred an ice-cold lady, one whose inhibitions he could overcome. Oh yes, undoubtedly that was the answer, he would need to be the boss.

She was stupid to waste her thoughts and emotions on him when reality meant Nick. Yes. When Steve finally left the hospital she must give more serious consideration to Nick's proposals. She wished she knew what he actually meant when he said he wanted her with him always. He told her he loved her and she knew he fancied her, but he had never asked her to marry him. Perhaps he thought she'd take that for granted. Yes, that was it. As Mrs Trowbridge she would lead a comfortable, fun-filled life. How Tessa would envy her! She knew that Nick would always put money first in his life, but that would also benefit her and she would be able to have those things she had missed out on when she was young. In fact the more she thought of it the more attractive it seemed.

She took more care than usual with her appearance when she went to meet him that evening. She washed her hair and gave it a gold rinse, put a smear of blue shadow on her eyelids and a new coral lipstick on her mouth. Then she chose to wear a dress she had bought for special occasions, a pleated sky-blue crêpe.

Nick looked even more handsome than usual in a white shirt which contrasted so well with his tan and gleaming jewellery. They looked at each other in mutual admiration before kissing affectionately.

'Shall we eat first or go down to the promenade?' he asked.

'I think I'd like the walk first, it's such a beautiful evening. Just look at that sunset!'

The western sky was turquoise blue streaked with molten gold and cast reflections over the rippling sea.

'I must drop in at my place for a few minutes, I need to pick up some letters,' Nick told her. 'Okay?'

The view from his window was superb, the cliffs of the coastline with the hills behind, the lights that were appearing in the houses, and over all the sun-streaked sky.

Nick poured some wine. 'To us,' he said, his brown eyes smiling into hers. 'Let's sit outside for a while.' He opened the door which led on to the balcony.

'What a lovely site you've chosen, Nick, it couldn't be better,' Hilary said dreamily.

'You like it?' He seemed pleased. 'I had my eye on it for over a year. So when it came on the market——' He raised his shoulders and spread his hands. 'If someone in the business can't get what they fancy, then who can?'

She nodded. 'You love your work, don't you?'

'I'm good at it. It's selling, and I like that.' He leaned across and kissed the tip of her nose. 'I'm going to sell you the idea of living with me.'

'We'll have to see about that, won't we?' she smiled, still wondering what his real intention was.

'You like to play hard to get, don't you? Well, let me tell you I enjoy a challenge.'

She stopped him as he was about to refill her glass.

'I need to have my wits about me when I'm with you,' she told him. 'Let's go and have that meal, it's unwise to drink on an empty stomach. Or was that what you were banking on?'

Nick clicked his thumb and forefinger. 'She's rumbled me! Never mind, Nick old son, better luck next time.'

Laughing, they left his apartment and climbed the leafy hill to the restaurant hand-in-hand. He stopped outside to buy a copy of *El Pais*.

'I must keep an eye on my adverts, they cost me enough.' He riffled through the pages of the newspaper as they sat at their table. 'Here we are, half a page with photographs.' He studied them carefully to make sure the wording was correct. 'They'll do.' He was looking for somewhere to put the paper when Hilary asked if she might have it.

'That's something I miss—English newspapers,' she said.

'This one isn't English——'

'I know, but I can look at the pictures.'

'You'll need to learn Spanish when you work for me, you wouldn't get far without knowing the language.'

She smiled and raised her eyebrows. '*When* I work for you? You do take a lot for granted!'

As she folded the paper to put under her chair Hilary saw the word 'Costella' in the stop press.

'What does it say about Costella?' She passed it to Nick.

He stared at it. 'A coach crash.'

'A coach crash? But that's——' Her heart missed a beat.

'And here's a list of casualties. I hope to God it doesn't include any of my punters. Imagine that for bad luck!'

Hilary jumped up and went to read the names over his shoulder. Apart from most of the others, she read 'Wendy Smith.' She pointed at it with a shaking finger.

'What does it say about her?' she asked anxiously.

Nick read silently through the list of names. 'No, no name I recognise. What were you saying?'

'Wendy Smith—her name is there. What does it say against it?'

He read with intolerable slowness. 'She's among those killed. Oh, poor old Wendy! That's tough.'

'Killed? But she was with Steve. Does—does—oh, tell me what it says!' Hilary implored.

'What I told you—a coach crash and a list of casualties.'

She was staring frantically at the page. 'Oh, look——' She pointed to the name S. Sanders. 'That's him. Tell me——'

She suddenly realised that contrary to what Nick had implied he could not read Spanish well. Snatching up the paper, she looked around the tables, then went up to a middle-aged, obviously English lady who was reading a book.

'Please—forgive me, but can you read Spanish?' she gasped.

The lady looked up from her book. 'Oh yes, I can read Spanish. What is it you want to know?' She took the paper from Hilary's shaking hands. 'Oh, another coach crash—how dreadful! This one went over the side of a road near Costella. It's dangerous there, I know it well, there's a sheer drop to the side. *Quatro muerto*—four people killed. A child trapped beneath the coach was dug out uninjured by an English doctor who was a passenger, Dr Sanders, who is now in St Peter's Hospital, Costella. Then there's a list of the casualties. Do you want the names?'

Hilary slowly shook her head. 'No, thank you,' she whispered.

'Do you know any of them?' the woman asked.

'Yes. Dr Sanders works in the hospital here and Wendy Smith was with him. She was killed.'

'Oh, my dear, how dreadful! Can I get you a drink?'

'No, thank you—I'm with a friend. Thank you so much for reading it for me.'

'Don't mention it. You know, they should erect barriers on that road, accidents are happening all the time.'

Hilary returned to her table and sank down on to her chair.

'Wendy's dead and Steve is in hospital—it doesn't say why. Oh God!' She covered her face with her hands.

Nick laid a hand on her shoulder. 'Don't be upset, honey. That's why I didn't read it to you.'

'He might have been killed!' she moaned.

'And I might have been a millionaire if I'd been luckier. You mustn't worry about might-have-beens. The fact is he's in hospital. Well, heck, he's dealing with other people who are in hospital every day. It'll be nothing to him.'

'But being with Wendy when she was killed . . .'

'Nasty business. But I don't think he was all

that keen on her. If he was, then he didn't show it. But then he seems a bit of a cold fish.'

'Oh, you haven't got any feelings!' Hilary snapped angrily.

'You bet I have! If I'd seen the name of one of my punters on the list of those killed I'd have done my nut!' Nick laughed. 'What you want is something to eat and a stiff brandy. That'll buck you up.'

'I'd like the brandy, but I couldn't eat anything,' she said.

After she had felt the warmth of the spirit she felt her strength returning. So poor Wendy had been killed, but there was so much to be thankful for. Steve was alive!

'Thank you, Nick,' she said gratefully. 'I feel much better now. I think I'd like to get back to the hospital, though, if you don't mind.'

With surprising understanding and gentleness he left her at the hospital gates with just a friendly kiss on her cheek.

'You'll feel better in the morning,' he told her. 'Try and get some sleep.'

CHAPTER NINE

HILARY spent an almost sleepless night. When she occasionally dozed off she would start up in horror, sweat pouring from her, as she visualised the coach full of passengers toppling off the road and Steve staring at her through the window as it somersaulted down and down the cliff and he was gone for ever.

At three o'clock she got up to make some hot milk, but sleep still eluded her. She deliberately pushed away the thoughts of the accident, refusing to let her mind return to it. But she had to think about something, and now it was Nick and her indecisions that went round and round in her head. She was thankful when her alarm went off unnecessarily at six o'clock.

She got out of bed as tired as when she had got into it. On seeing her reflection in the mirror as she passed she gave a shudder of horror. She looked terrible, her face was so pale as to be almost sallow and her usually wide eyes were narrow slits sunk into dark hollows. She knew she must do something to improve matters, for Pat was a firm believer in everyone, staff and patients alike, looking their best. She believed it to be a stride towards recovery. Indeed, she would bully lackadaisical patients into making use of the services of the visiting hairdresser.

So Hilary took a shower, dousing her face in cold water, alternating with hot, until some colour returned and her eyes looked brighter. She need not have bothered, because nobody on the ward was in the least concerned with anything other than the accident, not even their own ailments.

When the newspaperman's sing-song voice was heard coming towards the ward proclaiming his arrival everybody had their money ready and greeted him eagerly as they bought up most of his papers, even though they were in Spanish.

'Can any clever person read Spanish?' Hilary asked the patients.

Surprisingly it was Anne who was the most fluent, and there was absolute silence as she read and translated from the paper.

'Costella coach crash—English doctor rescues child trapped in debris. Hold on a sec while I work out the next bit. Yes—well, it says the coach went off the road and came to rest on some rocks on the cliffside. Several of the passengers were thrown out. Four, including the driver, were killed. Survivors helped to release the passengers who were trapped or injured. Oh, here we are, here's the bit about Dr Sanders. It says "Carola Pilla, a six-year-old girl, was trapped beneath the coach. An English doctor who was also a passenger on the coach, thirty-three-year-old Dr S. Sanders, risked his life by clawing his way through debris to set her free. She was not seriously injured, but the doctor was later taken to St Peter's Hospital, Costella, with severe lacerations to his hands. Within minutes of the rescue the coach overturned and fell to the bottom of the cliff." Then there's a list of casualties. That wasn't an exact interpretation but the best I could do. I learnt my Spanish from my boy-friends, didn't I? And they deal more in words and actions than in the written word!'

Immediately the talking broke out, voices mingling as nobody listened to what anyone else was saying. But there was a general and wholehearted agreement that what Dr Sanders had done was wonderful, just what you'd expect from him, and thank goodness he and the child were safe before the coach fell to the bottom of the cliff.

'So he's thirty-three,' said Anne, as if it mattered. 'Just the right age for me. Don't let anyone discharge me until he's back—now that my tube is out I'm hoping he'll fall for my fatal attractions.'

Strangely, it was her facetious remark that brought normality back to the ward, and although in many cases it needed thermometers to be placed under tongues to stop the talking, patients gradually remembered that they hadn't slept well, nor had their bowels opened, and pain-killers were requested and given. Life was back to normal.

Hilary was in Pat's office having morning coffee. After the usual discussion regarding patients' progress, reaction to certain treatment and general condition, the talk inevitably turned to the accident.

'Poor Steve hadn't had a holiday for as long as I can remember, and now this had to happen.' Pat shook her head.

'It's dreadful, but could have been so much worse,' Hilary said with feeling. 'I'm glad they were able to enjoy their holiday before this happened, though it doesn't seem important when you think of poor Wendy.'

'Nobody has mentioned his young lady, which seems sad,' commented Pat.

'Well, I don't suppose they knew her, really.'

'No.' Pat held up the coffee-pot. 'More coffee? I only saw her once myself when she called here for Steve and I told her where she would find him. As I remember, she seemed quite a nice-looking girl.'

'Yes, she was. I met her a few times in the restaurant over the road, when she came in with Steve. She was studying medicine.'

'Was she? Then they'd have had a lot in common, and he could help her with her studies.'

'Yes. He took her on this tour because he wanted her to see as much of Spain as possible while she was here.'

'He's like that,' Pat said fondly. 'He's always thinking of another person's good.'

Hilary felt guilty and taken aback. Why hadn't

she thought of it in that way? Why had she always considered that he was bossy?

'What about his hands, Pat?' she asked. 'I mean, for a surgeon they're so important. Wouldn't it be dreadful if——' She couldn't go on.

Sister Prowse patted her arm. 'A surgeon's hands are vitally important, we all know that, but they're not everything. Even if he could never operate again he has other skills, he wouldn't be lost to the profession. Just be thankful, my dear, that he's alive. It could so easily have been different.'

Hilary looked warmly at Pat. 'Oh yes, it doesn't bear thinking about. But what about the rest of him? Is it just his hands or—or more than that? And then there's the loss of Wendy . . . what he must be going through. I do so wish he'd been brought here, then we would all have been here to look after him, see he didn't feel all alone . . . '

Pat stared ahead thoughtfully. 'Costella isn't so far away. The buses run there. When have you got time off?'

'Me? I've got three hours off this afternoon, but that's not long enough to——'

'I'll find out the times of the buses and we'll see what we can arrange. There's no one who'd complain about you going to see how he's doing. Take an early lunch and I promise not to notice what time you get back. Okay?'

Hilary did a most unexpected and unprofessional thing. She leaned across and kissed Pat's cheek.

'Thank you, Pat, you really are the kindest person in the world,' she said fondly.

As she waited at the bus stop every minute seemed like an hour, and she worried in case she had missed it. But at last it came along and to her surprise was only three minutes late. She found the journey horrific, for it was on just such a winding road with a sheer drop to the side that the accident had happened. She clenched and unclenched her fists as the coach swerved from side to side as she had done in her nightmares. Had it not been for that it could have been a pleasant trip, because the scenery was beautiful. But the trees and bushes seemed to come closer and closer, then fade into the distance, only to rush forward again. She remembered this feeling well from her first day in the operating theatre. Surely she wasn't going to faint as she had there? If she did, would they put her out on the roadside and leave her stranded there? She didn't know whether to laugh or cry at her imaginings, but when at last they came to a road with buildings on both sides she felt a tremendous relief.

The bus stopped practically outside St Peter's Hospital and she got out on legs that felt as if they were made of elastic. After a difficult conversation with a hospital porter who knew more English then she did Spanish, she managed to discover that Steve was in a side room off the men's medical ward. She stood outside the white-painted door, breathing deeply, silently praying that he would be all right. Reluctantly, dreading what she might see, she quietly opened the door a little and peeped in.

Steve lay in bed, apparently asleep, his heavily bandaged fists outside the sheets. Hilary tiptoed closer, not wanting to disturb him, and sat on a chair beside him.

There was a dressing on his forehead, a deep scratch on the side of his nose and a swollen abrasion on his cheek. This was the first time she had had the opportunity of looking at him closely. His dark hair, usually so neat, was tousled and his eyelashes lay on his cheeks like two brown curls. His eyebrows tilted slightly at the outer corners—she had never noticed that before. In repose there was no sign of arrogance on his face, indeed his mouth looked gentle and vulnerable. A dark stubble had grown on his chin and instead of his usual crisp shirt he had on a collarless, hospital issue striped nightshirt. Hilary's heart swelled with love for him. He was like a little boy who had fallen off his bicycle and hurt himself. Instinctively she leaned forward and gently kissed his cheek, and had she not been afraid of waking him she would have drawn him close to her. Automatically her eyes had closed. When she opened them she found to her utter dismay and embarrassment that she was looking straight into his blue ones, that were only inches away. She drew back, her cheeks burning.

'Hilary?' he said, a doubt in his voice.

She gave a guilty smile. 'Hello, Steve. Forgive me, I was just kissing you better, you looked like a little boy. How are you feeling?'

He squeezed his eyes several times, then opened them wide. 'As if I'm dreaming. It's those wretched pills they give me. I said I didn't want any.'

'They say that doctors make the worst patients. *You* will have to do as you're told for a change,' she said with a smile.

'Did you come all this way just to gloat?' he demanded wryly.

'No, I'm here on behalf of Pat and all the others. We want to know about your hands. How are they?'

Steve held up his huge bandaged fists. 'Heavens be! Are they mine?'

Hilary grinned, happy that he seemed so much better than she had expected. 'Well, they're certainly not mine. And unless you've got someone hidden in your bed we're the only two here. But seriously, what's the damage?'

'I hope you mean "the extent of my injuries". Mostly superficial, but a couple of fractured bones. I never realised before how many things you need your hands for. I'm sure I'll be more understanding to patients with disabilities in future,' he said ruefully.

'You're always very sympathetic to them,' she

said. 'What about the rest of you? Have you any other injuries?' she asked anxiously.

'Nothing lethal, a few cuts and bruises.'

Hilary knew quite well that his physical injuries would be as nothing compared with the heartbreak of losing Wendy. She was going to find it difficult to speak to him of it, but she knew that she must. Biting her lip, she stared down at the bedcover.

'I—I'm dreadfully sorry about Wendy,' she said.

Steve made no immediate reply, and she flicked him a quick glance. His face looked drawn and his eyes filled with pain as he stared straight ahead. After what seemed a long time he said,

'Thank you. Of course, you'd met her. She had everything to live for. I would far rather it had happened to me.'

'Oh no!' The horrified reply sprang unbidden to her lips. But he didn't appear to have heard her.

'She was studying hard to become a doctor and it was my idea that she came here for a holiday, I thought it would do her good. It was my idea that we took that trip. If only I hadn't!'

Hilary opened her eyes wide. 'Steve, you know better than I do the futility of saying "if only". Accidents will happen and there's nothing we can do to stop them. And we certainly shouldn't blame ourselves when we didn't cause the accident—you know that.'

'We can only pick up the pieces,' he said with a sad smile, because that was a much-used expression in the hospital. 'Now I'm sure you didn't come here to listen to me moaning.'

'I came because everyone is anxious about you and they want to know when you'll be back.'

'Fairly soon, I hope. I have arrangements to see to about Wendy and many letters to write.' He made an impatient gesture. 'There I go again! It'll have to be phone calls to make. But I want to be able to return to St Margaret's before I finally leave.'

'So—so you'll definitely be leaving?' Hilary had a feeling of blank dismay.

'Oh yes. I came on a two-year contract. They won't want me after that.'

She thought miserably of how empty the hospital would be when he had gone. It would be bleak and hold no attraction at all, and suddenly she knew quite certainly that she could not stay there.

'I shall be leaving too,' she told him impulsively.

'You will? That's been a short stay, just a holiday. Are you tired of sunny Spain already?'

'Oh no, not of Spain, far from it,' she replied.

There was a satirical gleam in Steve's eyes. 'So you're having a permanent holiday, is that it? You think that's better than working?'

She recalled Sister Denver's acid comments and immediately needed to contradict him.

'No. If you remember, I had my holiday earlier. Now Nick—Mr Trowbridge has asked me to work for him.'

Concern darkened his eyes. 'I can hardly believe you want to give up nursing to sell properties. Pat speaks very highly of your work.'

Hilary swallowed hard. Even Pat's pleasant company could not compensate for the loss of Steve's presence.

Nick says it's foolish to spend so much time working in the hospital when I could be out with him, most of the time, in the sunshine.'

'But, my dear girl, life spent lying in the sun would become intolerably boring,' he warned her.

'I wouldn't be doing that, I'd be working, visiting properties with clients, that sort of thing.'

Steve lay back with his eyes closed for a while and she thought he might have dozed off, but suddenly he looked at her intently.

'Could you manage financially? Forgive my asking, but at the hospital you have free accommodation——'

Before he had finished speaking Hilary had blushed scarlet. How could she tell him that she would be sharing Nick's apartment? She had no need, for she saw by the expression on his face that he had grasped the situation. To her utter embarrassment he just continued to stare at her and wait for her to speak. The silence lengthened.

At last he shook his head almost imperceptibly. 'Don't do it, Hilary, don't do something I know you would regret. If you really dislike working in the hospital go back to England. Find somewhere else.'

Her embarrassment turned to anger. Anyone would think he owned her, telling her not to do this, not to do that! It didn't enter his stupid head that it was because of him that she wanted to leave. He just liked bossing people about, no matter what Pat's opinion was.

'You hate to think someone is enjoying themselves, don't you? Don't sunbathe, don't work for a happy-go-lucky fun-loving man, go on working in a hospital for all the hours God gave us, preferably back in a cold, grey country. You're a sadist!'

Pinpoints of light shone in his eyes. 'And you, unless I'm greatly mistaken, are a girl who wouldn't be happy settling for second best. I believe you to be a girl of principles, and I think you know what I mean.'

She turned her head aside, unable to face him as she said hesitatingly, 'It—it's not what you think. Nick says he loves me.'

His voice was low and serious. 'Don't confuse "I love you" with "I want to marry you". That might suit some girls—but would it be right for you, Hilary?'

She moved uncomfortably. 'So why do you think you know me so well? And why shouldn't he want to marry me? Have I got two heads or something?'

'For the simple reason that he's a playboy type. He's good-looking and has more than his fair share of charm, they're his passport in life. If he wants something or someone he'll not let conscience stand in his way over the methods of getting them.'

'So what's wrong with knowing what you want and going all out to get it?'

'Nothing, nothing at all. Unless in so doing you harm someone else.' Steve's voice was low and throbbing as he went on, 'I don't want that someone to be you.'

Hilary had a great longing to lay her head on his chest, despite the awful nightshirt, and to know that he would always be with her to care for her. But in her heart she knew that he would be just as considerate of any girl he considered to be in a hazardous position. And it was that knowledge that hurt so much.

'I can take care of myself,' she said casually.

Steve gave a short, sharp sigh. 'What do you know about this fellow, apart from what he's told you? Has he got a wife?'

Hilary was taken aback. 'A wife? Why, no—he would have said. Anyhow, he's not the type to be m——' She stopped suddenly.

'Married? Is that what you were going to say?'

Of course it was, and they both knew it. But she denied the suggestion.

'I was going to say not the type to keep such a thing secret!'

Steve shook his head with a mixture of sorrow and impatience.

'You shouldn't be allowed out on your own, you haven't any worldly sense at all.' His voice softened. 'Please—please, Hilary, don't do anything you might regret.'

To cover her embarrassment at what he was implying she said flippantly, 'I expect we all do things we regret at one time or another.' She gave a false laugh. 'All except you, of course.'

He looked so furious that for a moment she was scared. She was on the point of making her escape when there was a knock on his door and a nurse entered carrying a large bouquet of flowers.

'Aqui flores para usted, señor,' she said.

Steve thanked her as he read the attached card. Then, as she closed the door, he exclaimed angrily. 'Oh, blast!'

Hilary looked from him to the flowers in surprise.

'They're beautiful. What's wrong with them? Doesn't the colour match your nightshirt?'

He gave her a withering glance. 'No, they're very beautiful, but a totally unnecessary gesture on the part of one of the passengers on the coach—or rather, her relatives.'

'That little girl's parents?' she asked gently.

He nodded briefly. 'So you heard about that. God knows what rubbish the newspapers said about it. Don't believe it, it's all lies.'

'I'm sure they said nothing that wasn't true. It was incredibly brave.'

'Yes indeed. That little girl was fantastic, not a moan or whimper or sign of fear. Every now and again she would smile at me. She should have had these, not me. You can't imagine how thankful I was when she was freed.'

Hilary wanted to tell him that *he* was the person she was worried about, that *he* was the one who was brave, but she knew she mustn't.

'I must go now,' she said. 'I've got a bus to catch.'

Steve nodded. 'Yes, of course. It was very kind of you to give up your time to come here when you could have been lying out in the sun.'

She was bitterly hurt by his words. How could he imagine that anything was as important to her as seeing him? Her eyes were wet and full of misery as she looked at him. Suddenly he leaned forward and taking her face between his bandaged hands he ran his lips across her mouth, then he kissed her, a long, lingering kiss that made her tingle with ecstasy.

She stood for a moment, filled with delight. He had kissed her!

His eyes were smiling as he said, 'You kissed me first, never forget that!'

Hilary turned to go.

'Give my best wishes to Pat and the others,' he said.

When she reached the door she looked back

to say goodbye. For a moment their eyes met and locked.

'Think over what I've said to you, Hilary,' said Steve.

She made no reply, but left to catch her bus.

CHAPTER TEN

STEVE Sanders was back at work, and once again the hospital seemed to come alive.

He held up swollen, scarred hands. 'They look more like a boxer's than a surgeon's, don't they?' he said with a wry smile.

Sister Prowse eyed him fondly. 'You don't need me to tell you they'll soon be better.' She gave a short laugh. 'That's the sort of remark you make to a child when it cuts its knee!'

He exchanged a grin with Hilary. 'Trust Pat to cut me down to size!'

'The trouble is,' Pat said thoughtfully, 'you'll be leaving us before then.'

Hilary felt a wave of depression. She had known, of course, that he was going to leave some time in the future, even soon, but now that it was just three days away if she could have stopped time moving on she would have done so.

'My two years have passed quickly,' said Steve.

'Will you be sorry to go?' Pat took a sip of her coffee.

'She's fishing, isn't she?' Steve laughed.

Hilary smiled. 'Will you, though?'

'Now I've got two of you at me! I'm looking forward to taking a short holiday, I feel I could do with it. And yes, it's always sad to leave friends. On the other hand, I enjoy a change.'

'You've no immediate plans?'

He shook his head. 'No. I'll wait and see what turns up.'

'Remember to keep Saturday free,' Pat warned him.

'Saturday?' He frowned.

'It's your party, for goodness' sake! We'd look proper Charlies if we held a party for you and you weren't there.'

Steve looked uncomfortable. 'It's very sweet of everybody and I do appreciate it, but you could have done me a favour and scrubbed the idea.'

Hilary silently agreed with him. The thought of the party filled her with dismay. She could imagine the farewell speeches, the toasts, the tributes. Nothing would induce her to go to that, for she knew she would be fighting back tears.

'I don't think I'd have been very popular if I'd done that. Anyhow, it'll be a lot easier for you to say goodbye to them all at a party than having to ferret them out one by one only to find you'd overlooked someone. Don't you like parties?'

'If it's someone else's I can take it or leave it, but I don't relish one just for me,' he said with a shrug.

The telephone rang. When Pat had answered it she said, 'We've got an emergency admission, an asthmatic. Will you see to the bed, please, Hilary?'

The curtains were drawn and the bed ready by the time the patient was wheeled in. She was a Mrs Rowley, a middle-aged woman who was wheezing badly.

'I'll get you some extra pillows, you'll find that it helps if you can sit upright,' Hilary told her. 'And now I've got to ask you some questions. I'll try not to be too long.'

The woman nodded breathlessly. 'Yes, all right.'

When she had done Hilary took her temperature, pulse and blood pressure.

'Thank you, Mrs Rowley, that's all for now. The doctor will be with you in a few minutes.'

'Nurse!'

'Yes, Ivy?'

A patient sitting out beside her bed was pressing her hand against her ribs.

'They're hurting, Nurse. I don't know where to put myself for comfort.'

'I know. Bruised ribs are very painful and you've nothing to show for it. But I'll have a word with the physiotherapist and get her to bring along a heat lamp and see if that helps. Mind you don't sit too close to it. Would you like a pain-killer?'

'I'd rather see if the lamp helps first, I'm not one for taking pills.'

'Righto then, I'll see if I can get the lamp. But what I really think would be best is a heated kaolin pad because you can put that right on the painful spot. The trouble with that is that it takes twenty-four hours to heat up, but I'll mention it to Judy.'

It was a fairly busy day that went quickly, and Hilary was looking forward to meeting Nick in the evening. She was giving more thought to his plans for the future now that the hospital would soon have lost its appeal.

'Sam and Viv are arriving on Saturday, you'll like them,' Nick assured her.

Saturday! They couldn't have timed it better. Here was her excuse not to go the party.

'They're the ones from California, aren't they?' she asked.

'That's right. They've been over there three years and love it. I'm looking forward to taking you over there, showing you things that will make those wide eyes even wider. You'll just love Disneyland. Every little girl should see it.' He patted her cheek and laughed.

The music was pleasant, the meal excellent, and the wine made her feel relaxed. If she did as Nick wanted this would be her normal way of life.

He was even more attractive than usual tonight, happy because he had done some profitable deals that day.

'I might open an office in Los Angeles,' he told her. 'We could spend a part of each year over there. How would you like that?'

Hilary knew she should be saying that as usual he was taking too much for granted, but she didn't want to. It was all so tempting, she would go places and see things that otherwise she never would. And when she had children they would be able to have things she never had. They'd be like the children who lived by the lake.

Her thoughts went back to those childhood days. She could still see those privileged children, and Tessa and herself leaning over the dividing fence watching them and playing their makebelieve games. As a child she had been envious of those others, but now, reviewing it with adult eyes, she wondered whether they had, in fact, been happier than Tessa and her. A smile spread over her face as she recalled the delicious smell of baking when she returned home from school and her mother's welcoming smile. She remembered the happiness she felt when her father brought home an early spring flower, a snowdrop or primrose, and gave it to their mother. Or sometimes he would have a small bird or injured animal in his large gnarled hands for them to care for. Always in cold weather there was a blazing fire fuelled by the stack of logs in the outhouse. Hilary shook her head. Those other children were more likely to have been the deprived ones.

'What are you thinking about? Nice thoughts of me?' Nick took her hand in his.

She shook her head. 'Not this time. I was thinking of my childhood.'

'Good God! Can you remember that far back?' he asked teasingly.

'Beast! It's not so far back as yours is. What sort of a childhood did you have, Nick? Was it happy?'

His face went blank. 'No,' he said.

'Oh, Nick, why not?' she asked sympathetically.

He raised his shoulders and spread his arms. 'You asked me if I'd been happy and I said I hadn't. Now I'm not going to rake up old memories just to satisfy your curiosity.'

Hilary looked hurt. 'I want to know everything about you, and where better to start than when you were young?'

'That's your trouble, honey, you think too much about the past and the future. It's now that counts. I'm happy now, I'm not grumbling.' He squeezed her arm. 'I'm happy now because I'm with you.'

Much later she told him, 'Dr Sanders is leaving the hospital at the end of the week.'

'Oh yes? Has he got over the loss of his girlfriend?'

'No, I'm sure he hasn't, it's so soon. He doesn't mention it as far as I know, but I can see he suffers silently,' she said sadly.

'Suffers silently? What have you been reading? He knows it's no good crying over a dead dame,' Nick said flippantly.

'What a horrible thing to say!' gasped Hilary, turning aside.

He cupped her chin in his hands and turned her face to his. 'That saying is as old as the hills.'

'I've never heard it before.'

'You must have heard that it's no good crying over spilt milk?'

'Yes, I've heard that.'

He spread his hands and smiled. 'There you are, then. It's the same thing.'

She gave an impatient sigh, yet she knew it was no good expecting Nick to behave like other people. Now that she came to think of it, she herself had given but little thought to poor Wendy, who somehow seemed almost a stranger, someone apart. But for Steve it would be quite different, and she had noticed that he seemed quieter and at times she had seen a look of infinite sadness on his face and had longed to hold him close and comfort him.

'See you Saturday, then,' said Nick after he had kissed her goodnight.

'Yes. But not here, Nick. I'll meet you outside the restaurant. What time shall we say?'

'Half seven, and don't run away if I'm held up—you know how it is.'

'And what,' Sister Prowse asked her the next day, 'are you going to wear at Steve's party? Have you got something really pretty?'

Hilary felt guilty, almost as if the excuse she

was going to give was some story she had concocted.

'I won't be able to go to it,' she said. 'I've already promised to meet some friends of Nick's who are arriving from California.'

Sister Prowse looked bleak. 'But you knew we were having this party for Steve, we've been planning it for some time. You really should come.'

'Well, the dates just happened to clash, there's really nothing I can do about it.'

'Don't you like Steve?' demanded Pat.

'Oh yes, of course I do, very much.'

Pat frowned. 'These friends of his from California, your Mr Trowbridge will see them more than the once, won't he?'

'Maybe. I don't know.' Then the truth came tumbling out. 'The truth is I—I wouldn't like to be at Steve's party, knowing it was for the last time. That I was seeing him, I mean.' Hilary flushed, realising that she had probably said too much. 'What I mean is that I hate saying goodbye to people, to anyone. Don't you?'

Sister Prowse nodded slowly. 'Yes. Yes, I do understand. Ah well, it can't be helped, I suppose.'

Mrs Rowley was continuing to cause concern over her asthmatic condition and was having courses of physiotherapy to help her to cough and expectorate.

There were two new admissions, an elderly man with a slight stroke which had affected his speech and right arm and a woman with a varicose ulcer which might later require a skin graft but at the moment was being treated with a bandage of zinc paste.

Despite the sunny weather there was a minor epidemic of sore throats, chiefly amongst the staff, which made Hilary wonder whether really hot weather was as healthy as the cold spells they had in England. Germs probably thrived in warmth.

Saturday arrived, and although Hilary wasn't going to the farewell party she felt depressed. She couldn't summon up any enthusiasm at the prospect of meeting Nick's friends and she had not even decided what to wear. In any event this Viv would no doubt put her to shame with up-to-the-minute American fashion.

Sister Prowse replaced the receiver and stared into space, a frown creasing her forehead. Then a gleam came into her kindly eyes.

'Hilary, I'd like a word with you when you can manage it,' she said.

'Yes, Sister.' Hilary entered Mrs Rowley's blood pressure on her chart and put away the sphygmomanometer. 'Your inhaler is just here, Mrs Rowley, if you should need it.'

She glanced around the ward to see if she was needed, then joined Pat in her office.

Sister Prowse looked distressed. 'Oh, Hilary my dear, I don't know how to put this, but I've just heard from Nurse Waites and she's gone down with this throat infection. It's no good expecting her to come in or she could pass it on to everyone else. The point is, being Saturday it's too late to get a nurse from the bank. So—' she glanced ruefully at Hilary, 'I expect you've guessed what I'm going to say.'

'Yes, Sister, you want me to stay on.'

Pat nodded. 'I'm afraid so. And I know how you were looking forward to meeting those friends from America. I'm really sorry.'

Hilary smiled at her reassuringly. 'That's all right, I'm used to this sort of thing happening. We've just got to put up with it, haven't we? I wonder if I could use your phone to let Nick know, please? I can't just let him down.'

'Of course.' Pat pushed the telephone towards her.

Hilary was greatly relieved when her call was taken on an answering machine; she had felt cowardly about explaining to Nick, who she knew would not be pleased.

Pat smiled gratefully. 'You're a good girl. I'll see they send over some sherry and a few bits and pieces. We'll have a little party on our own.

'And much nicer, too,' said Hilary.

She could not even pretend to herself that she was disappointed at having to stay on duty. Here she was away from the sadness of the party, and of having to act heartily with Nick's friends.

As it turned out it was quiet on the ward that evening. True to her word, Pat had a tray sent across with a third of a bottle of sherry, some chicken and mushroom vol-au-vents, fish sandwiches and some cream cakes.

'This is great, much better than being over at the party, and I bet we've done better food-wise than the rest,' smiled Hilary. 'But Pat, all this talk about me missing the party, what about you? I thought you liked parties. Especially this one which you helped organise.'

'Well, yes, I should rather like to have had a peep. I tell you what I'll do—as it's quiet I'll nip across for a short while if you'll hold the fort. Would you mind?'

'That's a great idea. You do that, Pat. And don't hurry back, I'll be all right.'

'Okay, then. Keep an eye on Mrs Rowley, and if you need me, here's the number.'

Hilary wondered how Nick and his visitors were doing. She knew he would be annoyed that she had let him down once again, but conversation-wise she doubted if she would be missed. They would have a good time without her. Tentatively, like touching a sore tooth, she let her thoughts go to the party. Would Steve be dancing, and if so, who with? Would he be feeling at all sad that he was leaving? Would his thoughts be with Wendy, his lost love? Would he—would he notice that she wasn't there and wonder why? No, his thoughts would be with Wendy. He had hidden his feelings over the whole wretched affair—that, she supposed, was part of his training as a surgeon. It would be no good showing emotion when others were depending on you. Bossy, that was what she had called him, and now she hardly knew why. He certainly had the courage of his convictions, but was that being bossy? She couldn't even remember why she had felt so furious when he had told her not to lie out too long in the sun. There was surely no harm in telling her that? Oh yes, she knew why she had reacted in the way she did, it was because he had criticised her when she had wanted him to admire her. And she still did. Sister Denvers had shown her to be spoilt and useless in front of him, and that hurt still remained with her. She asked herself why she should care, and unwillingly admitted that it was because she loved him, and she knew now that she always had. What she didn't know was why. He had always been polite, friendly and caring, but that was all. Now Nick was affectionate and demanding and promised her so much. But in her heart she knew that nothing Nick could give her would amount to as much as just one loving kiss from Steve. At that thought she closed her eyes and felt a sweet thrill flow through her body.

A sudden sound in the ward sent her hurrying to Mrs Rowley's bedside. She was gasping and wheezing and her face was congested. Pausing only to make sure she was using the inhaler, Hilary hurried to the office and phoned Sister Rowley. Then she checked that the oxygen cylinder and mask were in good working order should they be needed.

She heard the lift doors open and close and the sound of footsteps as Sister Prowse and Steve both hurried into the ward. Steve examined the patient and patted her shoulder reassuringly.

'I'll give you something—just a little prick—and it will make you feel much better.

'We'll give her some aminophylline and keep a close watch on her,' he told Pat. 'She should be all right.'

'Yes, Dr Sanders. I'm sorry I left her,' Pat said.

He smiled at Hilary, a smile she treasured, and said, 'You left her in good hands.'

Outside the ward Hilary asked how the party was going.

'You go over and see for yourself. Now that Mrs Rowley is settled I'll be able to manage without you. And night staff will be on duty very soon.'

Hilary looked at Pat accusingly. 'Oh no—no, really I'm not dressed for a party,' she protested.

'You look very nice to me,' Steve told her.

'There now, that's all that matters, isn't it?' said Pat, meaning well, Hilary never doubted.

Unwillingly she followed Steve to the lift, staring speechless at the floor. When they were outside the hospital Steve said, 'I heard you had a prior engagement—with Nick Trowbridge, I suppose?'

'Yes. But I had to cancel it.'

They stood for a moment in the warm night.

The sky was dark blue and studded with stars. From the doctors' reception hall came the sound of music and the hum of voices.

'Don't you want to go over to him now?' he asked. 'It's not all that late.'

She felt an almost overwhelming desire to cry because he didn't care. He didn't want her at his party.

'Yes,' she said, too brightly, 'I'd like to do that.'

She started to walk away, knowing that he still stood there. Then she came back. 'I'd forgotten—I probably won't see you again, so I'll say goodbye and good luck. It's been good knowing you.'

She hurried away before her tears could fall, so she didn't see the hand he held out to her.

Once out of sight she hid in the shadow of some bushes while tears rained down her cheeks and she shook with sobs. Then, when they had subsided, she went to her room and to bed.

CHAPTER ELEVEN

'HAVE you met Steve's replacement yet?' Pat asked Hilary the following Monday.

Hilary shook her head, knowing that whatever the merits of this new doctor, he was fighting a losing battle as far as she was concerned, because nobody could take Steve's place.

'Then here's your chance,' said Pat under her breath.

The doctor who came into the office was very young with a thatch of ginger hair, a heavily freckled face, light blue eyes and a wide smile. Hilary hardened her heart. He was going to be popular with the patients, she was certain, because of his friendly manner. But she would rather the newcomer was disliked, or at best, tolerated, for she wanted Steve to go on being missed by everybody.

She had guessed right. After his ward round the patients brightened up immediately. The king was dead; long live the king.

As Hilary tended the patients and saw to their needs and listened to their problems a part of her mind was occupied with her own affairs. She became increasingly certain that she wanted to leave this hospital and decided not to hesitate any longer; she had been putting it off too long. So she wrote a letter to the Senior Nursing Officer saying that she wanted to leave. Her heart thumped as she dropped the letter in the box, but as she walked away she experienced a feeling of freedom such as she had not enjoyed for a long time.

She would be seeing Nick tonight, and between now and then she really had to make up her mind what her future plans were to be. From now on dithering was out. As she saw it, there were two ways around the boulders in the stream of her life—either to join Nick and enjoy the benefits that his money and his company could bring, or return to England and begin all over again the search for a vacancy in another hospital. The choice seemed simple enough. On the one hand was sunshine, warmth, comfort and fun; on the other was cold, grey weather and long hours of arduous work if she could get it. There must be something odd about her that she could even hesitate. Tessa wouldn't have seen any problem at all. Was it too late to model herself on her sister?

So much for telling herself that dithering was over. By the time she met Nick Hilary still hadn't made up her mind.

He was in a bad mood. 'I'm tired of being let down by you,' he said, his eyes unsmiling, his lips compressed.

'I know. I'm very sorry about that, but when

you work in a hospital that's one of the things you have to put up with.' She was about to tell him that she had decided to leave, but stopped herself. She wanted to wait for a more favourable moment.

'I would have taken someone else to make up a foursome if you'd let me know in time,' Nick went on. 'As it was, I had to turn up alone looking a proper wally.'

'I told you as soon as I knew. How were Sam and Viv?'

He frowned. 'You mean Sam and Darleen.'

'You said "Viv", I'm certain, because I know someone else with that name.'

'You're way off course. Sam's with Darleen now. She's cute—I could fall for her myself in a big way,' he said casually.

'So Sam's divorced?' Hilary looked at Nick in surprise.

'Divorced?' he laughed. 'Sam's not into marriage, and a damn good job too, with all the alimony he'd have to fork out. He's too smart for that.'

Steve's warning sounded in her ears. 'What about you? Do you believe in marriage?'

He raised his shoulders and spread his hands. 'Why not? If I lived in the Middle East I'd have my four permitted wives and lots of plump little concubines. I wonder if there's an opening there for an estate agent?'

Hilary didn't feel like joking, she wanted a serious answer.

'Wh—when you said you wanted me with you—were you asking me to marry you?' She felt herself tense with embarrassment.

'Honey, you're always worrying about something, and you mustn't do that. Enjoy yourself now. Come to me and I'll give you a good time. If we're happy, then maybe marriage, maybe not. What does it matter?'

So Steve had been right—of course! Nick hadn't meant marriage. He wanted her for a time until he met some cute girl he could 'fall for in a big way' and she would be cast aside, even if she still loved him. In the same way she believed he would have no scruples if a wealthy widow came along; he would always put money first in his life. And she would be left with nothing.

Suddenly she realised that charming though he could sometimes be, and excellent company, he was not the one for her. They were totally different. Maybe he was right in getting what he could out of life and enjoying it to the full, and she was wrong. But she knew she could never change, nor really want to.

As if someone had ripped a veil from before her eyes she saw that Nick and what he stood for was like last year's tinsel, glittering but tarnished, whereas the work and the good that Steve did was pure gold. Why hadn't she seen that before? Now she had no fear that Nick could persuade her to go to him.

'I handed my notice in today,' she told him boldly.

For a moment he looked wary, like a cornered animal, then he was smiling.

'So you're coming to me. That's super, I knew I'd get you in the end.' He kissed her as he had never done before, his tongue penetrating her mouth, his hands caressing her body. 'What are we waiting for, honey? Lets go to my apartment right now.'

Her treacherous body was tempted as he pressed her possessively to him. Then, disgusted with her weakness, she dragged herself away.

'No, Nick, I'm sorry, but you've got it wrong. I'm returning to England,' she gasped.

'To England?' he repeated disbelievingly.

'Yes. I—I got fed-up with the hospital.'

'To hell with the hospital! What about me? Why aren't you coming to me?'

Hilary shook her head. 'I just don't want to,' she said regretfully.

His eyes narrowed as the smile vanished. 'I get the picture. It's that doctor, isn't it? You could hardly wait for that other girl to be in her coffin before you stepped in, could you?' He laughed contemptuously. 'And you pretending to be such a prude!'

Hilary was horrified by his cruel remarks. 'You're wrong—I'm not going to him. I don't even know where he is,' she ended mournfully.

For an awful moment she thought he was

His face went blank. 'So she's gone to that estate agent.'

Pat looked surprised. 'I don't know if that's her intention eventually—perhaps it is, but she didn't mention it. She's flying to London today.'

'What time?' he demanded.

She frowned. 'Let me see now, I think she said her flight was at one-thirty, but I can't be sure.'

Steve looked up at the clock over the ward door, then he was hurrying away, calling over his shoulder,

'Goodbye, Pat!'

'Your books, Steve—you've forgotten your books!' she cried. But he was already in the lift and the door had closed.

Time was running out. At Malaga airport Steve hurriedly asked if there were any spare seats on the flight that was about to leave for Heathrow and was told there were several. He boarded the plane at the last minute. He had taken too much for granted, most probably Hilary had left on an earlier flight, so he looked around without much hope. Then he saw her, a slim figure, her fair hair tied up in a ponytail, her face looking wistfully out of a window. There was a vacant seat beside her, so he stood watching her for a moment.

Then he said, almost in a whisper, 'May I sit here?'

She gave a slight nod. Then something about the voice made her turn suddenly. She stared up at him unbelievingly. Seeing him here was a dream come true.

'Steve?' she queried.

'Hilary,' he said, and sat down beside her.

'I thought you'd gone back home ages ago, after you had your party.'

'I stayed on here while my hands were mending,' he told her.

'But fancy being here today, on the same plane as me! I bet you didn't expect that,' she smiled.

He looked down at her fondly. 'Then you've lost your bet—and I expect it's the first one you've ever made! I went to the hospital to speak to you and Pat told me you'd just left. So here I am, chasing all over Spain after you. I hope you're flattered.'

'Indeed I am, and puzzled too. Whatever did you want to say that was so important?'

His smile faded and a frown took its place. 'I know what I want to say, and I'm afraid I can guess what your reaction will be. But please believe me when I say that I only have your welfare at heart. I can't stand by and see you make a mess of your life. I had to see you again, try again to persuade you——'

'But I——' she interrupted.

'I know what you're going to say, that it's no business of mine.'

'That hasn't stopped you giving me advice before,' Hilary retorted.

'This Nick Trowbridge is bad news, Hilary,'

Steve said earnestly. 'I know you'll hate me for saying so, but I'm concerned for you. Don't take him seriously.'

She was both happy and angry. Happy because he cared enough to follow her here but angry because once again he was telling her what not to do.

'Do you always expect to run the lives of everyone you meet?' she demanded crossly.

'I don't think so.'

'Then why pick on me? You've done that since the first time we met.'

'So I have,' said Steve thoughtfully.

'Well, you haven't the right,' she said crossly, wishing so very much that he had.

'But I care.'

'When you first told me not to lie out in the sun you didn't even know me. How could you have cared?'

He raised his shoulders in a bewildered way. 'That I can't tell you. All I know is that I cared that you shouldn't ruin your lovely complexion, and now I care so much more that you shouldn't spoil your life.'

At his words the anger inside her melted. Unthinkingly she ran her finger gently along a scar on the back of his hand.

'That's kind of you. But how can you be so sure I would be spoiling my life by going to Nick? It's only your opinion.'

He crossed his legs and half turned away from her. 'I hoped I wouldn't have to tell you, only I can't seem to convince you any other way. But did you know that he was seeing Wendy when we were both working?'

Hilary was incredulous. Nick had never mentioned Wendy; even when he heard of her death he had seemed indifferent.

'I'm sure it would only have been for a drink when they met by accident,' she protested.

Nick shook his head. 'I'm afraid not. He made a pass at her, promised all sorts of wonderful things if she'd team up with him. She told me, and I have no reason to disbelieve her.'

Shock and embarrassment made Hilary furiously angry.

'And so, because he tried to take Wendy from you, you're trying to take me from him. That's despicable!'

Steve held her hand firmly. 'Calm down and listen to me. There was no question of him taking Wendy from me—I didn't own her.'

'But you were hoping to. She was staying with you, and I suppose you thought that was all right. But it would have been wrong for me to stay with Nick. Why should it be right for you and wrong for me?'

He stared at her in amazement. 'What sort of a man do you think I am? Do you honestly think I was cohabiting with my half-sister? That's an obscene suggestion!'

Hilary's eyes opened wide. 'Your—what did you say?'

'My half-sister. I told you she was born when my mother remarried.'

'And you were sent to boarding school—yes, I remember. But I didn't know that was Wendy.'

'Never mind about that. I'm talking about Nick. So you do see why I'm so worried about you, don't you?'

'Yes. But I've been trying to tell you that I've finished with him and that's why I'm returning to England.'

'And you won't be coming back?'

She shook her head.

'Oh, Hilary, you don't know how relieved I am,' Steve said fervently. 'Wendy was well aware of Nick's charm, she said, but she was a level-headed girl and saw through him. For a start she didn't like the way he behaved with her when he was supposed to be your special friend. But it was different for you. I thought you were in love with him.'

'So did I at one time,' Hilary admitted. 'He's very amusing and great fun to be with.'

Steve smoothed back his already tidy hair. 'What went wrong?'

She frowned. She couldn't possibly tell Steve that he himself was the reason.

'It's hard to explain,' she said hesitantly.

'Try.' Steve waited. He was nearly always able to get patients to speak if he waited long enough, just looking at them. He looked at her now.

'Well—being with Nick was something like

living on candy-floss and ice-cream and fancy cakes. At first you feel you can't get enough of them, but gradually you don't want any more. That doesn't mean that I stopped liking him,' Hilary added hastily.

'But you didn't like him enough?' Steve suggested.

She thought of their last embrace when she had been so sorely tempted and of the night when they had gone out in a boat on the moonlit sea.

'I liked him a lot,' she admitted.

'So?'

She moved uncomfortably. 'You do ask a lot of questions!'

He gave a small laugh. 'That's an occupational disease. Unless I know all the facts I can't make a diagnosis.'

'So am I your patient?' she asked, turning to him.

He shook his head vehemently. 'Quite definitely you're not. Tell me why you decided not to go to Nick when you admit that you liked him a lot.'

Steve was bossy, there was no getting away from that. Here he was, ordering her to tell him what should be her own secret. Yet somehow she didn't mind any more. She wanted him to tell her what to do if that meant that he cared about her. Sitting beside him and having him talk to her, no matter what the subject, was blissful. Indeed, she wished the flight could last for ever.

'Well, Hilary?' He put his hand on her arm.

'Well—liking isn't loving, is it?'

'No. Liking can be a mixture of good companionship, mutual fun and possibly physical attraction.'

Hilary nodded. 'Yes, that's just how it was with Nick and me.'

'Love is much deeper, something which is still there when the physical attraction and the desire to have fun have gone. It comes from the heart and is for ever.' He paused. 'Some people never find that love.'

She knew she had found it, and much good it was going to do her. She loved Steve if he was bossy or kind or ill in bed unshaven and wearing a ridiculous nightshirt. She believed nobody else could ever take his place in her heart. But what good was that if it wasn't reciprocated?

'Have you?' she asked, knowing she would feel devastated if he said he had.

'Oh yes,' he replied.

She stared dismally ahead. 'So are you going to marry her?'

'I certainly hope so.'

'Good,' she croaked. 'I hope you'll be very happy.'

His arm slid around her body and drew her close, and she ached with desperate longing.

'That will be up to you,' he murmured.

'To me?' she frowned.

'As you aren't my patient I can tell you that I love you very much.'

He was teasing—he must be. But that was cruel. She twisted up to look at his face. He was looking at her as if he meant what he said. His eyes were dark and gentle and loving. Her heart started to beat so fast and so strongly that she could scarcely breathe.

'You love me?' she faltered.

She felt his cheek against her hair. 'Of course I mean you. I've loved you since I first saw you. Especially when you turned your back on me and I saw that it was already peeling.'

She jerked away from him. 'You beast! It wasn't!'

Steve ran his lips across her forehead. 'So I'm a beast and I'm bossy. And do you know what? I want to marry you.'

Something seemed to explode inside Hilary's head. 'Marry me? But why?'

He hugged her to his side. 'So that I can be beastly and bossy to you always,' he chuckled.

'Oh, Steve, I love you so very much. I never dreamed you could love me too,' she whispered.

'What a damn silly place for us to be, with an audience this size. I want so much to kiss you properly and hold you in my arms,' he told her.

Hilary gazed at him lovingly. 'And I want that too.'

Steve looked around at the other passengers

and shook his head. 'We'll have to wait until we're in the taxi.'

'Taxi? Why, where are we going?'

'To your home, of course. I want to meet your parents and in time-honoured fashion ask your father for his daughter's hand,' he laughed.

Her home? Her parents? She loved them dearly, but how could she take Steve there after what she had led him to believe about her background? If he had known what it really was he wouldn't have been interested in her, because he was a wealthy doctor with, according to Pat, a flat in an expensive part of London and the use of an apartment in the best part of Spain. His friends and colleagues would no doubt be married to girls from privileged backgrounds, and if he married her she might at times let him down. She'd told him she lived in a house set in acres of ground and with a lake. No doubt he thought her father was a stockbroker or something equally impressive.

Once again she was being punished for telling a lie, but this time the punishment was a broken heart. She almost wished the plane would crash and she be the only casualty. But that wasn't going to happen.

She couldn't let Steve go home with her. Yet if she didn't then this would be the end of everything that mattered. She turned to look at him for what might be the last time. Her eyes wandered slowly from his smooth brown hair, to the most beautiful eyes she had ever seen, to his mouth which she so longed to feel on her own and down the length of his body in the cream silk shirt and beige slacks. Then, as if drawn by a magnet, back to his face.

He looked at her with gently smiling eyes and kissed the tip of her nose.

'Forgive me,' he said, 'but I couldn't help myself.'

Hilary steeled herself to do what she knew she had to do. Rubbing her hand briskly across her nose, that tickled, she said,

'Oh, Steve, you're rushing things—you must give me the chance to speak to my parents alone first.'

He frowned. 'Do you mean that maybe they won't approve?'

She gave a false laugh. 'Well, you know what parents are. Quite wrongly they think I'm rather special.'

When they had gone through Customs Steve said, 'And I think you're special too. Let me come back with you and at least take my chance.' He sounded puzzled.

A taxi stopped for them and Hilary got in and closed the door.

'Another time, Steve,' she said.

The driver started to move off. Steve ran up beside it. 'Your address? I haven't got it.'

'Never mind. I'll get in touch,' she said with a wave. Then as the taxi sped on its way she let the tears stream down her face.

CHAPTER TWELVE

TESSA was becoming increasingly irritated by Hilary's melancholy.

'For heaven's sake, why didn't you shack up with that fellow you talked so much about last time you'd been to Spain?' she wanted to know.

Hilary shrugged. 'Nick? He wasn't the marrying kind.'

'Lots of men aren't—girls too. You could have had a good time with him. But look at you now. I swear you've lost a stone in weight, which you could ill afford, and as for your face—ugh! So what do you think you've gained by giving him up?'

'Not a lot,' Hilary admitted. 'But you know I'm not like that, and I can't change.'

'Well, I'll tell you something for free,' said Tessa. 'You'll not get another bloke for marriage or anything else unless you buck your ideas up.'

'Look who's talking! I haven't heard wedding bells pealing for you,' retorted Hilary, goaded by her sister's remarks.

Tessa smirked. 'Who wants wedding bells? Marriage is out of date. Except for people like you, of course.'

'Well, I've made up my mind to be a dedicated nurse. Lots of women are. My problem being that I haven't got a hospital to be dedicated in,' said Hilary, half-humorously.

'No, that's too bad. Have you any interviews lined up?'

Hilary nodded. 'Yes, I've got one today at a teaching hospital in London. I won't get it, of course.'

'No, of course you won't,' Tessa agreed briskly. 'You wouldn't get a job as a lavatory attendant looking like you do and in your present mood.'

'That's a nice sisterly remark!'

'Take my advice for what it's worth—give your hair a gold rinse. Now you needn't put on a lot of make-up because they probably like a well-scrubbed look. But wear a decent dress.' Tessa opened the wardrobe door and riffled through the dresses. 'Yours are sun dresses, aren't they? That's not quite the thing. Let's see what I've got.'

'Gracious, no! I couldn't wear one of yours.'

'Why not?' Tessa demanded.

'Because they're not my style,' said Hilary.

Tessa lifted out a black and white striped silk. 'Now a nun could wear this. See, it's got short sleeves, no plunging neckline nor slit up the side. You'd look smashing in that.'

'When on earth did you buy that?' queried Hilary. 'And why?'

'Well, we had a new curate, see, and I rather

fancied myself as becoming a vicar's wife one day.'

Hilary laughed. 'So what happened?'

Tessa grinned. 'He took one look at me and went into a monastery.'

Hilary held up the dress and was tempted. To wear any of the dresses she had worn in Spain would bring back unhappy memories. Trying on the dress she felt a new person. It was smart but modest, although she could well imagine it would look different on Tessa.

'Thank you,' she said. 'I'd like to borrow it, if you're sure you don't mind.'

'Wait a minute.' Tessa went to her drawer and took from a bulging cardboard box a red necklace, and foraging around found stud earrings to match.

'These are the finishing touch. And—keep still.' She applied some matching lipstick to her sister's mouth. 'See? How's that?'

Hilary had to admit that it looked good.

'So you be sure to wear it, and I'll leave my lipstick on the dressing table.'

'Thanks a lot, Tessa,' Hilary said gratefully.

'Okay. I'll send my account in later!'

Hilary waited with a number of other hopeful nurses in the hospital, which must have employed over a thousand nurses. She would have preferred to work in a smaller hospital where she could get to know her colleagues, but nevertheless, if she was lucky enough to be taken on here she'd be over the moon.

She had been to enough interviews not to feel too apprehensive. She knew the sort of questions they would ask, and she'd either know the answers or bluff her way through. She knew that personality counted, and she inwardly thanked Tessa for her kindness, for she felt far more confident and outgoing than usual.

It was a long wait, and by the time it was her turn the panel seemed bored with the whole procedure and not terribly interested, as if they had already decided who they were going to appoint and this was all a waste of time.

When she got out into the street there was a feeling of anticipation and liveliness in the air; the pavements were crowded with visitors and the shops were colourful. She glanced in at the windows and shuddered at the prices as she made her way to the station. As she passed Weymouth Street the name seemed familiar. Weymouth Street? Why, yes! That was where Steve lived. What was the number Pat had said? Six or sixteen? Hilary hesitated by the flower stall on the corner, then slowly turned into the street. It would be interesting to see where he lived.

There were several smart shops and then an impressive gate with numbers set on a panel by the side of it. Both six and sixteen were in this block. But there must be other blocks in the street. Hilary sighed and turned away. A flat in this street would cost a bomb. Steve was a very wealthy man.

It was rush hour in the tube and there was scarcely room to breathe, yet at each station more people crowded in. Then gradually as they reached the outer suburbs the train shed most of its passengers.

Hilary walked slowly through the park, stopping by an old brick wall to admire the roses that climbed over it. She remembered her father telling her that many years ago a queen who had visited the park on the occasion of its being opened to the public had snipped the stems of newly planted roses, saying the wall would be ruined by them. Apparently she had been wrong.

She felt, as always, the homely happiness as she went indoors. She could smell a fruit pie and knew it would be delicious. Apple? Blackberry? Gooseberry? It didn't matter which. She just hoped the family wouldn't ask her too many question about the interview, because there was nothing to tell. She pushed open the kitchen door and saw them sitting around the table, which looked inviting with the steaming hotpot and its crispy potato topping.

'Hello,' she said, flinging down her handbag.

A chair was pushed back and somebody stood up. After the bright sunshine the room seemed in darkness and she couldn't make out who it was. So she smiled at a dark shadow.

'Hello, Hilary.'

Her heart leapt. 'Steve!' she gasped.

Then they were all talking and saying how excellent the hotpot was. The room was bright enough now, but Hilary dared not look at Steve. She knew Tessa was flirting with him and she was glad, as it saved her having to make conversation.

'What a delicious tart. Are they your own blackberries?' Steve asked.

'Father picked them up by the lake, a lot of them grow there. I always make some blackberry jelly, it sees us right through the winter.'

'And blackberry wine. That's good stuff,' said Mr Wilson. 'I've got a few bottles put by, you must try some before you go.'

When they had finished the meal with cups of strong tea, Steve said,

'I'd like to see this lake I've heard so much about. Will you take me there, Hilary?'

'Yes,' she replied, staring at the tablecloth.

'Will you need a coat?' Steve asked as they were leaving.

'Maybe,' she said, and went to get her anorak. But Tessa streaked up the stairs before her and handed her a bright red cardigan.

'And the best of luck,' she winked. 'He's absolutely super, and if you let this one slip away I wash my hands of you!'

'So what game are you playing?' demanded Steve when they were well away from the house.

'What do you mean?'

'You know quite well what I mean,' he said sternly. 'You said you'd get in touch—and don't give me the "I lost your number" yarn, because I won't believe you.'

'All right. But how did you know where I lived?'

'Because I cared enough to find out. I went to your old hospital and made enquiries.'

'So now you know,' she said flatly.

'Know what?'

'That I don't live in a house set in acres of ground with a lake, but in a workman's cottage.' Hilary forced out the words.

'So? You do live in acres of land, and I presume there's a lake or why are we walking this way?'

'Oh, you know what I mean! I was pretending to be something I wasn't. Even if I cross my fingers when I tell a lie I'm always found out,' she said sadly.

'And a good thing too. What makes you think you have the right to pretend that your parents, your background, are different from what they are? Surely you aren't ashamed of them, because they're splendid people, and I envy you your home. Never, ever do such a thing!'

'You're bossing me again,' she said, smiling, because she felt so happy.

'And I always will,' threatened Steve. But all she felt was sheer delight.

'There's our lake,' she said, as they glimpsed the water between the trees.

Some ducks squabbled at the water's edge and a swan sailed majestically past them, spurning them.

'This is where Tessa and I played when we were young,' she told him.

'Yes. Boating and sailing, you told me.'

'That wasn't true either. What we played were games of makebelieve, when we told each other what we'd do if we lived in one of those big houses over there.'

They sat on the grass beneath the trees and she told him about the things she and Tessa had longed to do.

'Just a little girl's dreams,' Steve said fondly.

Then he lay back and drew her close. His arms were around her and his mouth was playing games with her, kissing her in unexpected places so that she laughed and squirmed and tried to wriggle away. Then he took her mouth more passionately than she had ever imagined. She could scarcely breathe, but she would have had it no other way. He held her so close she could feel the hardness of his body through the thin silk dress, and feelings she never knew she possessed made her long desperately for something more. She wanted him closer, even closer.

'I want you,' he murmured hoarsely. 'Now, Hilary, beside the lake that nearly separated us.'

'Oh, yes, Steve, I want you too,' she murmured, not knowing exactly what he had meant.

She shivered as his hands touched the skin beneath her dress and she was convulsed with desire. She could hardly wait for—she knew not what.

And then—the sheer bliss, the ecstasy, the release of all her tensions mingled with his and became the most wonderful experience of her life. Now she belonged to Steve for ever and ever.

As they still lay together, spent now, but contented, he said,

'One day I'll buy you one of those houses across the lake and our children will have all those things you wanted. Will you like that?'

'Oh yes,' she said, 'I'd love to have one of those houses.'

But now it wasn't because of the things they could give their children which, after all, they might not want. It was because she would always be able to look out over this magical spot beneath the trees where she and Steve had become one in the most wonderful act of love.